TROUBLE AT MOON PASS

TROUBLE AT MOON PASS

BURT ARTHUR

CUTTING EDGE

ISBN-13: 978-1-954840-78-2

Published by
Cutting Edge Books
PO Box 8212
Calabasas, CA 91372
www.cuttingedgebooks.com

TROUBLE AT MOON PASS

CHAPTER ONE

OF DARKNESS, DEATH
AND DEFIANCE

IN THE darkened hollow between the shadow-draped, sprawling, humpbacked hills and the silver stretch of river stood a shack, an indistinguishable mass of blackness that rose from the ground and reached vaguely for the dim night sky. Inside the shack half a dozen men slept deeply. Behind the shack, in a small, crudely fashioned corral, a dozen weary mules huddled together for protection against the chilling wind.

Somewhere in the vast darkness beyond the corral, off in the nearby hills, the echoing, mournful wail of a lonely coyote arose and drifted across the rangeland with the wind. From farther off a wolf took up the cry. Hearing in the wolf's cry the ageless challenge of a deeply feared enemy, the coyote abruptly ceased his lamentation and slunk off into silence.

The silent wind raced breathlessly over the moonlit, silvery river. A troop of horsemen, almost as silent as the wind, threaded their way along the river bank, turned inland and spurred at a quicker pace toward the darkened shack. The last man in line wheeled when he came abreast of the corral, pulled up and lowered the bars and rode in among the mules.

"Git!" he ordered in an undertone.

He slapped one mule across the rump. The animal backed away hastily and collided with his neighbor. The horseman kicked his right foot free of its stirrup, edged his horse closer and drove his booted foot into the mule's ribs. The mule grunted and scurried past him and loped out of the corral.

"G'wan!" the man said gruffly. "All of yuh!"

The other mules trotted out. The rider dismounted and picked up a rock and hurled it after them with considerable accuracy. There was a brief bawl of pain, and the mules ran faster, their hoofs clattering away into the night. The man vaulted back into his saddle and rode around to the front of the shack. There was a farm wagon off to one side; three men dismounted and disconnected the shaft and used it as a battering ram against the door. With a loud splintering crash, the door jerked off its hinges and fell in. A yell rose from within the darkened shack. The men dropped the shaft and scrambled away, jerked out their guns and whirled around.

"Come outa there!"

There was no answer.

"Awright. Give it to 'em!"

Guns flamed and roared with sudden and deafening thunder; a hail of lead sprayed and shattered the front of the shack. Both of the shack's front windows, one on either side of the doorway, were blasted away. Gunsmoke swirled up and around the doorway.

"Hold it!"

There was a minute's wait; then a burly man poked his head out the doorway.

"Come outa there, you!" they called to him.

The burly man stumbled out. He was barefooted and wearing only his long underwear, which was far from white even against the black background. The leader of the raiders eyed him, grunted and stepped forward. The others crowded forward, behind him, their guns raised and ready. Moonlight ran along the lifted, menacing barrels.

"You other fellers in there—yuh better hustle out here while yuh still got the chance!"

Five men, none of them fully dressed, all of them sleepy and bewildered, tumbled out. They lined up beside the burly man.

"I'm givin' you just two minutes to git inter your clothes," the raiders' leader said coldly. "That's a better break than you deserve, but I'm willin' to give it to you. Now git your things. One of you at a time, an', mind you, no tricks. Then come out here again. Make it lively."

When the six men had put on their clothes and returned, the leader addressed them again.

"This is your last warning," he began curtly. "If we find you around here again after tonight, what'll happen to you, you won't live to tell your grandchildren about."

He paused and cleared his throat fiercely.

"This here is cattle country," he went on, "an' we aim to keep it for cattle. What's more, nobody's gonna build any railroad across these here plains 'less we say he can, an' you oughta know there ain't much of a chance of us agreein' to that. You might remember what I'm tellin' you an' repeat it to the maverick who hired you. Now the river's over there. See it? You just foller it north till you hit your main camp. And when you git there, if you got any sense a-tall, you'll ask for your wages an' hightail it away from here while you still got your health. Now, git goin'."

The six men turned without a word and plodded toward the river. They tramped along in silence until they reached the grassy bank, when they halted and furtively looked back. The raiders had set the shack on fire, and it was burning with a crackling, hissing sound. Bright, eager flames swirled around it and lapped at the wooden walls with an all-consuming greediness and leaped up swiftly toward the roof. One of the men cursed. His companions mumbled under their breaths. They watched until the shack was nothing but ashes and charred, smoking timbers. Then they turned and trudged off.

An hour later they halted again, this time for a brief rest, and looked back. There was a black plume of smoke in the graying sky. As they watched it, tight-lipped and sullen, the smoke plume curled more thinly and vanished on the wind, as if extinguished by some giant's breath.

It was not full daylight when a train of ten heavily laden mule-drawn wagons rumbled onto a level stretch of ground and braked to a creaking halt on the rolling prairie. The cargo, long delayed and long overdue, consigned to the main railroad camp, included a varied assortment of much needed material. Spikes, rails, tools, kitchen supplies and track-laying equipment were stacked in the wagons.

The tired, steaming mules were unhitched. Their heads bowed and their quivering legs widespread, they did not stir despite the removal of their harnesses. Their equally fired drivers had to lash and drag them out of the traces. After they were fed they were tied to the big wheels of the wagons for the night.

A campfire had already been started. It was burning brightly and cheerfully. The teamsters gathered around it; just looking at it made them feel better. They squatted down on the ground, cross-legged like Indians, eating ravenously of a make-shift supper of bacon, flapjacks and coffee. When they had finished, they lay back, resting on their elbows, some of them smoking in silence, others talking and exchanging tales of other jobs, chuckling as they recalled amusing experiences they had had.

Finally the talk died away; then, one by one, they climbed stiffly to their feet, yawned and stretched, picked up their blankets and crawled under the wagons, rolled themselves up snugly and went to sleep.

A sharp wind droned over the prairie, whined through the short grass and brush and raced away toward the south. The campfire burned brightly for a time, then, unattended, died quietly out. From a distance, armed and patient men watched the camp. Undetected, a band of horsemen had trailed the wagon trail since dusk and now, satisfied it was safe to attack, moved in. Shadowy figures left their horses and crept forward. Far down along the line of wagons a mule raised his head and brayed. A shadowy figure straightened, hesitated for a moment, then whirled and ducked behind the mule; but it was unnecessary. The teamsters were too tired to let a mule's senseless braying disturb them. There was a low whistle from one of the stealthy figures, and guns leaped into the hands of his companions.

"All right!" he yelled. "Git up outa there!"

There was no response from the sleeping teamsters.

"Wake 'em up, boys!"

The raiders needed no urging. They ran in, whooping and cursing, jerking off the blankets of the sleeping men.

"Git up. Git up there!"

A couple of the drivers awoke, rolled over to reach for their blankets and, finding them gone, blinked and stared with heavy, barely opened eyes at the men who stood over them; then with gaping mouths at the guns held steadily in their hands.

"C'mon. Haul y'self up outa there, yuh hear?"

Some of the sleeping men still did not stir. But a few more well-directed kicks brought a quick and complete response. The teamsters rolled out from under the wagons and dragged them-selves to their feet.

"All right, Foster," a raider called to the man in command of the party of horsemen.

"They all up now?" Foster asked.

"They sure are."

Foster strode forward. "Line up, you fellers," he said authori-tatively. "I got a few words to say to you."

The teamsters obeyed slowly and wearily.

"I'm givin' you a chance to get away with a hull skin," Foster began, "not because you deserve a break like that but because I'm bankin' on you havin' enough sense to do's you're told an' hightail it away from here. There ain't any railroad gonna be built 'round here. That clear? All right. Now get outa here. If we run into you again, you can figger out for yourselves what'll happen to you. That's all. Get goin'."

The silent, sullen men hitched up their belts, turned slowly and trudged away.

CHAPTER TWO
A MAN NAMED DORAN

SQUAT, paunchy Matt Burnham, President of Western Railways, paced the floor of Captain Jim Reynolds' office. He had refused to take the chair beside the latter's desk by the eloquent gesture of kicking it out of the way. Reynolds, chief of the railroad's police, eyed him patiently.

"Damn it all, Jim!" Burnham broke out finally. "This thing's getting out of hand altogether."

Lean, tall, gray of eye and tight of mouth, Reynolds nodded.

"So they're still raising hell with that spur you're trying to build, eh?"

Burnham abruptly stopped his pacing.

"You bet!" he said heavily. "And the bank's getting nervous and won't let us have another blasted nickel till the spur's finished and in operation. But getting back to those thick-headed cattlemen, they're driving our laborers away, burning our property and destroying our supplies. Next thing you know they'll start blasting at us, and with hot lead, too. That'll be the payoff."

Reynolds' steely eyes glinted.

"Then it's time we got down to cases before it comes to gunplay," he said quietly. "Engineers and laborers aren't much hand at gun throwing, you know. They won't stand a chance against those cowpunchers, most of whom are top hands with a shooting iron."

"You telling me? You suppose I don't know that? Jim, I'm stumped. I'm dropping the danged mess right in your lap."

Reynolds grinned sarcastically. "Thanks—that's sure decent of you, Matt. And what am I supposed to do with it?" he asked.

Burnham grinned back at him. "Better figure that one out for yourself," he retorted. "You used to be able to handle things before without asking for help or advice. Or maybe you've forgot those days?"

"No. Don't think I ever will."

"Well?"

Reynolds dropped back in his chair. "What about the writ you got the court to hand down? Isn't that supposed to give you the right of way? Have you made any use of it, or did you forget about having it?"

Matt Burnham's lips thinned. "Huh!" he snorted. "For all the good that writ's done me, I could've done without it. The county attorney at McCloud—a mean polecat named Sears—won't pay any attention to the writ. And there's nobody can stand up to him and make him. We tried to get the sheriff, a mangy critter named Ike Boone, to do something about enforcing the law, but he and Sears stand together on this thing, and they're standing mighty pat. I'm about ready to bust, Jim."

"I can see that," Reynolds said.

"Well, maybe you won't be so smart-sounding after you've tangled with those McCloud polecats personally," Burnham retorted. His eyes gleamed suddenly. "This ought to be mighty interesting to watch. Maybe they'll knock some of that cockiness out of you."

Jim Reynolds' eyes twinkled.

"Maybe. But I'll bet you anything you like, Mister President of Western Railways, they'll know they've been in a fight," he said. He paused for a moment. "Give me an idea of the set-up, Matt. Are any of the ranchers around McCloud on your side, or are they all set against you and the railroad?"

"Oh, there's a couple willing to let us show them that we can do what we claim we can for them. The trouble is, Jim, there aren't enough of them to back us up. The bunch opposing us would sooner die than let a railroad come busting across their range-lands. They're too doggoned bull-headed to try to figure out how much help we can be to them. The whelptailed mavericks just won't listen. They just say 'No' and they keep saying it, and that's the end of it."

Reynolds nodded.

"I know the kind, Matt," he said. "Met some of them down in Texas, and I learned that when they won't go for a thing—hell, they just won't. Arguing with them gets you nowhere. They just gotta be showed. You gotta get tough. It looks 's if we'll just have to adopt some of the same kind of treatment we used down Texas way and give them some of the same kind of medicine, too."

Burnham shrugged his shoulders.

"Whatever you say, Jim. You're the doctor."

Reynolds frowned.

"I know—only prescribing for 'em ain't all I'm going to have to do. I'm going to have to get them to *take* the medicine, too."

"Uh-huh. And what do you aim to do first?"

"Remember a big blond kid named Doran?" Reynolds asked. "Dan Doran?"

Burnham rubbed his chin reflectively.

"Doran?" he repeated. "Doran? Oh, yes. Didn't he work for you when you were head of the Texas Rangers?"

Reynolds nodded. "Yes. Only he isn't a kid any more. He's full grown and a pile of man."

"What about him?"

"Dan was the best man I had. He could outsmart and out-fight anybody he ever went after. He come in to see me the other day, foot-loose an' job-hunting. I put him on, figuring something might come along I could use him for and, doggone it, it sure has. This job's made to order for him. If those hellions up McCloud way are looking for excitement, Doran'll be only too glad to accommodate them."

"All right. If he's all you claim he is, what are we waiting for?" Burnham demanded.

Jim Reynolds climbed stiffly to his feet.

"Keep your shirt on," he said. "You've been messing around with that damned spur up at McCloud for more'n six months and it still ain't even been started. So don't go getting impatient now. Dan'll be on his way to McCloud today. That good enough for you?"

Burnham grunted.

"You got any suggestions to offer?" Reynolds demanded. "Anything that might be helpful to him?"

Matt Burnham shook his head. "No," he said. "None. This is your funeral, mister. I don't aim to horn in on it and hand out any advice so's you can blame me when something goes wrong. I'm wise to you. From now on I'm just setting back and looking on."

Reynolds grinned fleetingly. "Maybe I ought to tip them off at McCloud that Hell-on-Wheels Doran is coming this way," he said. "Wouldn't want to have them trampled underfoot when he blows into town and starts mowing them down."

Reynolds looked up and gave him a withering stare.

"Think you're being funny?" he demanded. "All I have to say is, when Doran hits McCloud those two mavericks you mentioned—that feller Sears and that side-kick of his, Dan'l Boone—"

"Ike Boone," Burnham corrected him.

"Huh? Oh, yes, Ike Boone. Should have known nobody named Dan'l Boone could be a skunk. Anyway, when Doran hits McCloud they better find themselves a couple of good storm cellars. Things'll be coming their way, and they won't be bouquets, either."

Burnham grinned broadly, turned and started out, only to halt again in the open doorway.

"Might offer you one suggestion," he began. "When this hellcat of yours swings into action he might come up for air for a minute and look up a rancher named Ben Miller."

Jim Reynolds grunted.

"Thanks for the tip. 'Course it probably won't be worth much; still I'll see that Dan gets in touch with this Miller before he goes into action. Anything else?"

"No."

Burnham jerked the door shut behind him and plodded away. The hallway that led to the street door was dark. He collided forcefully and suddenly with a tall, rangy citizen who literally towered above him.

"Watch where yuh're goin', Shorty," the tall man said in a curiously gentle tone. "Yuh're liable to get hurt trying to climb over grown folks."

Matt Burnham drew himself up to his full five feet.

"Why, you long-legged so-an'-so," he sputtered. "I ought—"

The tall man, hands on his hips, looked down at him. "Go on, mister, tell us what you oughta." Burnham could not see the tall man's face, but he was certain the other was smiling at him in the same curiously gentle, mockingly patient way that he had spoken.

Burnham glared up at him. In spite of the poor light he could take in the man's broad shoulders, his muscular arms and big capable hands. He noticed the brace of heavy Colts which hung low against his thighs.

"S'matter?" the tall man demanded tauntingly. "Lose your tongue, mister? I thought yuh had a little speech to make us."

Matt's lip curled. He gritted his teeth on his pride, circled around the tall man and stalked out. The tall man grinned, turned slowly and watched him for a second or two, turned again and hitched up his belt and sauntered along the hallway until he came to Reynolds' office. He opened the door and poked his head inside. Reynolds was seated behind his desk, frowning and staring off into space.

"I'll come back when yuh ain't so busy."

Reynolds looked up.

"Huh? Oh, it's you, Dan. Come in."

Doran stepped into the office. He was as tall as Reynolds, just as lean and lithe and perhaps a bit broader across the shoulders. He closed the door behind him and leaned back against it. He shoved his hat back from his eyes.

"Just bumped into a little squirt comin' outa here, Cap," he said casually. "Funny little feller. I sassed him some, an' he got all bristly."

Reynolds laughed. "That was Matt Burnham. Your boss, jughead."

Doran's eyes widened. "Burnham?" he repeated. "Yuh mean the feller that owns this outfit?"

Dan Doran whistled. "Boy! Ain't that somethin'? Sassin' th' boss! Reckon that means I'm fired."

"I wouldn't worry too much about that," Reynolds said softly. "Nobody's goin' to fire you except me, and right now I need you. But one day, you'll find yourself speak-in' a piece to somebody who's going to answer you with a couple of bullets. Sit down."

Doran relaxed. "Got somethin' good lined up for me mebbe?"

Reynolds nodded. "And how, Dan. And you're going to have to handle this job all by yourself."

Doran grinned. "That's fine. Then I won't be able to complain about anybody gettin' on my nerves," he said. "Where do I go an' when?"

"To McCloud, Dan," Reynolds answered, more gravely. "Figger you can pull outa here today?"

"Right now, Cap, if yuh say so. Don't have to do much packin' to speak of. All I own is right here on me."

Reynolds nodded, rose and came around his desk. Doran climbed lithely to his feet, and shifted his holsters. Together they turned toward the door. Doran halted there and waited while Reynolds, suddenly remembering his hat, wheeled and strode to a cabinet in the corner of the office, jerked open the cabinet door and took out his hat.

"Yuh seein' me off?" Dan asked with a grin.

"I'll ride part of the way with you," Reynolds replied. "That'll give us a chance to talk. Don't want to send you off half cocked and without knowing what you're goin' to find at McCloud. Come on, boy. Slam the door, will you?"

The white horse topped a rise and halted upon Doran's soft command. Below them, dripping downward gently, was a green and rolling valley.

The smell of fragrant sweet grass rode softly on the wind, and big shade trees stood green and nestling in the sunlight.

"Shore is nice country 'round here," Doran mused, half aloud.

He kicked his feet free of the stirrups and let them dangle against the flanks of his horse. He shifted in the saddle and made his seat more comfortable; he could feel his whole body relaxing. Then with startling suddenness a rifle cracked somewhere in that tranquil valley below. Instinctively he stiffened into an upright and alert position in the saddle. The white horse jerked her head up nervously. Doran's hands tightened on the reins.

"Easy, Bess," he said.

His probing eyes raced over the valley, searching it for a sign of a rifleman or the telltale puff of white smoke which always followed the discharge of a rifle. Presently he spied it. At that same moment he spotted a horseman, about a mile away, coming toward him at a rapid clip, lashing his pounding horse with a desperation born of fear.

Doran frowned resentfully at the sudden intrusion into his musing and into the outward serenity of the scene. Then, as he watched and wondered at the man's haste, three more horsemen hove into view. It was immediately obvious that they were pursuing the single rider. The rifle cracked a second time, and a bullet whined over the man's head in a wide miss. He flattened himself hastily against his horse's neck.

"They'll be shootin' for keeps next time," Doran muttered. "Wonder what it's all about?"

Two of the pursuers, spurring their mounts, bounded far ahead of the third man and rapidly cut down the distance between their quarry and themselves.

"Reckon it's all over now but the shoutin'," Doran said half aloud. "That feller's horse must be plumb done in, judgin' by the way those other two are catchin' up with him."

Now the two horsemen separated and overtook the single rider, ranging themselves on either side. One of them leaned out of his saddle and reached for the faltering horse's bridle. His rider, twisting suddenly, lashed out and struck the man full in the face. The horseman fell forward in his saddle. His mount slackened his pace and dropped back, but his rider, recovering with amazing swiftness, forced himself upright again, drove his spurs into his horse's flanks and sent him bounding away a second time. His companion edged his horse closer, grabbed the reins and jerked the pursued man's horse to a skidding, stifflegged halt. In another minute the other two men came pounding up.

The man who had been struck lost no time in returning the blow. He hit his captive twice, savagely, with his right fist. The man wilted and sagged in the saddle and finally fell to the ground. He landed on his left shoulder and toppled over. Doran frowned again and jerked the reins.

"Go 'head," he said sharply. "This looks like it might be int'restin'. Let's get closer to it."

Bess moved off. She negotiated the grassy incline that led to the valley with surefooted ease, quickened her pace when her dainty hoofs touched level ground again and flashed away. Doran was about forty feet from them when the mounted men heard the mare's racing hoofs, turned in their saddles and looked up. Dan checked his mount's pace to a jog and trotted up to them. The captured man lay in a limp heap between the three horsemen. Bess halted.

"Howdy," Doran said. He looked down at the sprawled figure for a moment, raised his eyes again presently and met the glances of the three men. Slowly he grinned. "That feller always do his sleepin' in th' daytime?"

One of the three men scowled. Dan noticed a tiny trickle of blood on his chin. The horseman wheeled his mount away from his companions' horses, edged him forward and halted again in front of Doran.

"Who're you?" he demanded.

Dan grinned again. "Me? Name's Doran if it means anythin' to yuh," he replied casually.

The man grunted.

"It don't," he said gruffly, "so yuh might's well mind your own bus'ness an' keep goin'."

Doran's easy, casual grin vanished. His lids dropped almost sleepily, veiling a steely glint that sparked up in them suddenly. When he spoke, his voice had a curious, purring softness.

"I aim to, mister," he said evenly, "only I don't like bein' pushed. Besides, when yuh talk to me yuh wanta put a smile into your voice. Sometimes I'm plumb mortified at how easy I rile up. What's that feller done to yuh, aside from beltin' yuh and spoilin' your disposition?"

The man flushed angrily. His lips thinned. Fresh blood surged out of a corner of his mouth and ran down his chin. His hand dropped suddenly toward the gun which swung against his right thigh. It halted with equal suddenness, abruptly and in mid-air as though an unseen power had gripped and stayed it. It was the sight of the heavy black Colt which had flashed so effortlessly into Doran's apparently relaxed right hand that caused him to hold his play. The blunt muzzle of the Colt gaped at him, yawned at his belly. He stared hard at it for a moment, and the muzzle seemed to grow larger. He jerked his head up. His hand relaxed, came upward again, slowly and evenly so that Doran could not misinterpret the movement, and came to rest on the horn of his saddle.

"That's right friendly," Doran said quietly. He looked past the man and glanced quickly but cautiously at the other two. They seemed to be satisfied just to be onlookers, rather than participate in the near-fray. He swung his gaze back to the man in front of him. "Yuh fellers lawmen?"

There was no spoken reply, nothing but a mute and significant sneer on the man's face. It was all the answer Dan needed.

"Figured you weren't," he said softly. "Maybe you'd best turn around an' get outa here."

There was no movement from any of the three. The heavy Colt snapped upward. Cursing, the three men gripped their reins, wheeled their horses and jogged off. At a word from the man with the blood-streaked face, they spurred their mounts and sent them racing away. Doran, motionless in the saddle, his Colt still upraised, followed them with his eyes.

"That's that," he muttered finally. "If those polecats are from McCloud, we oughta have a mighty int'resting time next occasion we meet."

The horsemen disappeared in the distance. Dan holstered his gun, dismounted and bent over the man on the ground.

CHAPTER THREE
MCCLOUD

"A LL RIGHT, pardner," Doran said.

The man opened his eyes, made a wry face and forced himself up on his elbows. He gave Dan a brief, fleeting glance and twisted around, looking for his captors.

"If yuh're lookin' for them other three fellers," Doran said casually, "they're gone. Hope yuh ain't disappointed. They seemed pretty anxious to talk with yuh."

The man turned again and dropped back on his elbows. His eyes probed Dan's face.

"Who—who are you?" he asked.

"Me? Oh, nobody in particular," Doran answered lightly. "I just happened to be passin'. I suppose yuh might say I kinda butted in when I saw yuh get walloped an' tumbled outa your saddle. Anyway, along I come, an' first thing I knowed your friends decided they had more important business somewheres else an' they just hightailed it away from here. Maybe I said something to hurt their feelings."

The man gave him a sidelong glance and shifted himself into a sitting position. Dan had already noted that he was fairly young, probably not more than twenty years old. He noticed too that there was a deepening, blood-red welt on his jawbone and another bruise directly under his left eye. This welt was beginning to swell.

"H'm," Doran said after a minute. "That shore is a beauty under yore eye, pardner. By tomorrow mornin' yore face is gonna be in full bloom. An' from the looks of that scrape 'longside your jaw, yuh'll find eatin' an' talkin' kinda tough."

He straightened up. The young man struggled to get up on his feet.

"Here," Dan said. "I'll help yuh. Gimme yore hand."

He caught the youngster's hand and hauled him to his feet. He stepped back, hands on his hips, and ran his eye over him. He noticed that there was a holster on the youngster's hip, noticed too that it was empty. It answered the unasked question as to why he hadn't tried to shoot his way to safety.

"How yuh feel, son?" Doran asked.

The youth nodded mutely. He ran a finger over his jawbone tenderly, then gingerly over the swelling under his eye.

"Who were those fellers?" Dan asked.

The youngster opened his belt, tucked his shirt tails into his pants and retightened his belt and looked up.

"They're from McCloud," he replied briefly.

"Uh-huh, an' the feller who belted yuh?"

The youngster looked ugly. "That was Foster," he said. "Dunno exactly what that polecat's s'posed tuh do fer a livin', 'cept that he seems t' have a heap tuh say 'bout things in town. Shore acts like he was the boss—leastways everybody seems tuh hop to it when he tells 'em to."

Doran grunted.

"Reckon he is the boss, then," he remarked. "So his name's Foster. I want to remember it for the next time we meet. What were they after yuh for?"

"Wa-al," the youngster began, "they're buildin' a railroad that's tuh connect Fargo an' Tonopah. McCloud stands between 'em. The connectin' spur's s'pposed tuh take a shortcut through Moon Pass." He hesitated.

"Uh-huh. An'?"

The youth moistened his lips.

"Some o' the ranchers," he continued, "are willin' tuh have the railroad come 'cross their grazin' lands. Others ain't. Them that ain't are doin' all they kin to line up the hull danged country an' fight the railroad."

"I see."

"Well, those who're willin' tuh give the railroad a try are havin' a helluva time of it. Their cattle an' their men are bein' run off. I was warned tuh quit my job, but I tol' 'em tuh go tuh hell. Y'see, mister—I work fer the Bar-M —that's Ben Miller's outfit—an' since Ben's the leader o' the ranchers who are willin' tuh play along with the railroad, we've been gettin' an extra dose o' strong-arm stuff. Anyway, Ben's been dog-goned good tuh me, an' I wouldn't quit 'im now no matter what happens."

"Good for you," Doran approved. "I've heard of this Ben Miller. I'll have to look him up one of these days."

"Yuh lookin' fer a job?" the youth asked quickly. "If yuh are, Ben'll be doggoned glad tuh have yuh, 'specially after I tell 'im what happened an' what yuh done fer me."

"Thanks, but I dunno for shore yet exactly what I'm goin' to do," Dan replied. "I just roll along mostly. Got an itch in my saddle, I guess. But if I decide to stay 'round here, I'll remember that. Which way yuh headed? If it's toward McCloud, I'll ride along with yuh."

The youngster shook his head. "I'm goin' the other way," he said.

"Oh. Then I'll be leavin' yuh here. Mebbe we'll be runnin' into each other again?"

"Mebbe. But don't forget what I told yuh 'bout the Bar-M, mister, if yuh decide tuh stay 'round here."

"You bet," Doran answered. He turned to Bess, caught the reins and vaulted into the saddle.

The youth stepped forward and thrust up his hand.

"Much obliged, mister," he said. Doran's hand came down to grip his hand. "I'm Bud Watkins. Folks call me 'Kid.' If yuh ever need a favor, just lemme know, willya?"

Dan grinned. "I shore will, Bud."

"Oh, yeah. Yuh ain't told me yore name."

"It's Doran—Dan Doran. So long."

"So long an' thanks."

Bess loped away. Doran twisted in the saddle and looked back. Bud looked up, waved and strode off toward his idling horse. Doran settled himself in his saddle.

"Let's go, Bess," he commanded. "I'm kinda anxious to see what McCloud's like. Seems to be quite a place."

The white horse lengthened her stride.

A stagecoach came lumbering out of McCloud as Doran neared the town. He jerked the reins sharply, and the nimble-footed mare swung off the trail to allow the stage ample roadway. The coach rolled abreast of them. The driver, a swarthy, mustached man, eyed Doran sharply as he passed. There was another man on the front seat, holding a shotgun across his knees. He raised his right hand in salute. Doran acknowledged the greeting gravely with a wave of his own right hand. Presently the stage, following the twisting road, disappeared, leaving a cloud of dust behind it. Dan guided the mare onto the trail again. Minutes later they were riding down McCloud's main street.

The town was a-hum with activity. Horsemen clattered along the street in both directions while men on foot cluttered up the narrow wooden sidewalks. Inquiring, questioning and appraising eyes turned toward Doran and the sleek white mare as they rode along, but Dan paid no attention. As a stranger in McCloud, he expected to be stared at. Bess, on the other hand, dominated by the inborn and persistent vanity of her sex, decided that it was she and she alone who was the object of all the attention, jerked her head up sharply and whinnied shrilly. Everyone within range turned and looked at her. Completely satisfied, she pranced on. Doran spied a sign far down the street—*Hotel*—and headed for it. He noticed that there was the usual preponderance of saloons in McCloud, drew rein in front of the hotel, dismounted and looked up at it with critical eyes.

The hotel was a two-story structure, weather-beaten and sun-faded and badly in need of fresh paint. Most of the other buildings along the street were equally shabby in appearance. Not exactly, Dan thought, a town that looked too prosperous to need the railroad.

Dan hitched up his sagging gunbelt, shifted his holsters, patted Bess' neck and sauntered across the wooden walk to the open doorway of the hotel. He looked in. A tiny lobby met his eyes. Off to a side was a narrow stairway that led to the upper floor. Beneath the stairs was a desk, and behind it a bald-headed man dozed peacefully and loudly. His chin rested upon his chest, and with each breath his head jerked up and came down again with a hollow thump. Doran grinned, drew out one of his Colts and strode to the desk. He hammered on it with the gun butt.

"Hey!" he yelled. "Wake up there!"

The clerk's bowed and nodding head jerked upward violently. His eyes popped open. They were red-rimmed and sleep-laden. They blinked and groped for a moment in confusion and bewilderment. They halted finally on the tall blond man in front of him, focused themselves upon him.

"Wha—what s'matter?" he sputtered.

"Yuh got any rooms?" Dan demanded.

"Fer you an' who else?"

Doran frowned impatiently. "For me," he snapped. "I'm kind of fussy 'bout where my horse beds down, but I don't mind bunking here. I've seen worse before and I likely will again."

The clerk frowned sourly. He gave Dan an aggravated stare, and mumbled under his breath. Yanking open a drawer below the level of the surface of the desk, he pulled out a huge key, glanced at the number on it and slammed it down in front of Doran. Doran was reaching for it casually when the man's right hand shot out suddenly and jerked the key away.

"One buck, mister," he said rudely. "In advance."

Dan shrugged. He dug into his pants pocket and produced a silver dollar and tossed it on the desk. "There's your buck."

The clerk grunted, scooped up the coin with his left hand, examined it, then shoved the key across the desk with his right hand.

"There's yore key."

Doran picked it up, turned on his heel and headed for the stairway.

"Hey!" the bald-headed man called.

Dan halted and looked back at him.

"Yeah?"

"Take off yore boots when yuh get inter bed," the clerk said coldly. "The sheet on the bed I'm givin' yuh was washed two weeks ago. Gotta keep it clean fer 'nother two weeks—see?"

Dan grunted an indistinct reply.

He plodded up the stairs, halted on the landing and looked at the key in his hand. It bore the number '4'. He looked up at the first door along the hallway. A huge, crudely fashioned '4' had been chalked upon it. He unlocked the door, pushed it open and stepped inside. He halted presently, his hands on his hips, and swept the room with his eyes.

"H'm," he muttered to himself. "Just about what I expected to find."

There was a small window on one side of the room. There was no curtain over it, nothing more elaborate than a torn, frayed and faded blind drawn halfway down the window. The lower half of the blind had been torn off.

"Wonder when that window was washed last," he muttered. "Bet it ain't been done since the place was put up."

His eyes ranged over the room. A single, iron-framed bed with tall posts stood just beyond the middle of the room. A faded, almost threadbare coverlet was spread over it.

Against the opposite wall stood a small table; on top of the table was a washbasin and a discolored pitcher with a black crack in it that ran from the top to within an inch of its base. Opposite the door and against the far wall was an armless and backless chair. It sagged curiously to one side. Doran looked at it again and saw that it had only three legs. Then he shifted his gaze back to the bed, spied something under it and bent down to get a better look. It was the missing chair leg. He shook his head, straightened up slowly, turned a bit and kicked the door shut.

He whipped off his hat and sailed it across the room. It landed on the chair, slid across the sloping seat and dropped limply to the floor. Dan unbuckled his gunbelt and dropped it on the bed, reconsidered almost immediately, picked it up again and hung it around the nearest bedpost. He unbuttoned his shirt and rolled up his sleeves and strode to the washbasin. He caught up the pitcher and looked into it. It was half filled. He poured the water into the basin, spied a small piece of soap beside the basin and proceeded to wash himself. He soaped his hands and arms, face and neck; and was liberally belathered when he heard the door open. He turned toward it and cursed when soap seeped into his eyes.

"Damn it," he mumbled. "Hey, clerk, where'n hell's the towel, or don't yuh have any in this joint?"

A towel came swishing across the room. It struck him in the face. He lunged for it, but it eluded him and slipped into the water-filled basin.

"Yuh dumb fool!"

His right hand groped for his handkerchief. He found it finally, yanked it out of his pants pocket and wiped his smarting eyes. He mumbled a curse under his breath, blinked once or twice and looked up.

"H'm," he muttered. "Company."

Near the bed and dangerously close to the post on which his gunbelt hung, two men stood, their thumbs hooked in their belts, fingertips poised within inches of their gun butts. A third man, big and broad-shouldered, his back turned to Doran, kicked the door shut and swung around.

It was Foster. The bloody smear was gone from his chin, but there was no concealing the cut itself—a deep, inch-long gash on his thick lower lip.

Dan shot a quick, sidelong glance at his own belt, measuring the distance to it and wondering if he could reach it before the three started blasting away at him. One look at their faces told him they hadn't come to offer him the keys to the city. The burly Foster, following Dan's eyes and sensing what was racing through his mind, pushed forward quickly, shouldering his companions aside; he reached for the belt and jerked it off the post.

He sent Doran a mocking, wordless grin and received a cool steady stare in return.

"Howdy," Dan said finally. "Would it be askin' too much to state yore business prompt-like? Or maybe I should offer yuh a seat."

Foster's eyes narrowed. "Shucks, mister," he said protestingly, "there ain't no call for yuh to use that tone on us. We're here to do yuh a favor."

Doran smiled ingenuously. "That's what I figgered," he said, his blue eyes dancing mockingly over their faces. "Go ahead—I'm listenin'!"

"Right," Foster said. "Y'see, mister—me an' the boys got to thinkin' 'bout yuh after we left yuh. We kinda got the idea that you an' McCloud wouldn't hit it off well together a-tall."

Dan's eyebrows arched. "That so?"

Foster coughed lightly behind his big left hand.

"Uh-huh," he said. "We decided that bein's yuh're a stranger, we'd do the right thing by yuh an' tip yuh off 'bout how downright unhealthy it is fer strangers 'round McCloud an' kinda suggest that yuh might find it—the climate an' everythin', y'know—more to yore likin' somewheres else. Do yuh foller me?"

Doran smiled again, perhaps a bit more easily than before.

"Shore do. Matter of fact, I'm follerin' yuh so close I'm surprised yuh ain' complainin' 'bout me breathin' down the back of your neck," he replied. "So yuh don't want me in McCloud, eh?"

"Yuh catch on to things fast, all right," Foster told him.

"I've been told that before," Dan said in full good humor. "Suppose instead of hightailin' it away from here, I decide to stay put. What happens then?"

One of Foster's men turned and looked at Foster. Foster winked and patted his holster significantly. The man laughed and turned around again. Doran frowned and rolled down his sleeves and buttoned his shirt, strode over and picked up his hat and clapped it on his head. There was a grin on Foster's face.

"All set?"

Dan nodded. The burly man backed to the door and jerked it open and held it wide. Doran sauntered forward, halting in front of him.

"Long's I'm takin' your advice, mister," he said mildly, "reckon I might's well go the hull hog an' take my guns, too, eh?"

Their eyes met for a brief moment. "Shore," Foster said amiably. "Here y'are."

He handed the belt over. Doran took it without a word and buckled it around his waist, gave Foster a brief nod and strode out.

CHAPTER FOUR
ACTION IN MCCLOUD

Donlin's Café was the most popular place in McCloud. It was never referred to as a "café" and only rarely called a "saloon." McCloud spoke of it simply as Donlin's and felt that that was sufficient.

Owned by a former cattleman, Donlin's catered to the sun-bronzed, swaggering, boisterous men who rode the open range, and to their employers whose ranches lay between Fargo and Tonopah. With McCloud located midway between these two larger towns and more accessible to most of the ranchers than either, it was natural that it should receive the patronage of the entire in-between region. Donlin, sizing up the situation, saw to it that every courtesy and every comfort was extended to the cattlemen. In return they made his place their headquarters.

The cowboys, who were more often broke than solvent, found Donlin a willing and patient creditor, amply endowed with tolerance and understanding. He gave them all the credit they wanted; offered them the run of his place and refused to allow their noisy horseplay to ruffle his calm.

There was a method to his madness. Donlin had made a study of pleasure and relaxation, and come to the conclusion that no man could enjoy himself properly and with profit to his host if he were continually plagued by the fact that he had but limited or meagre capital with which to finance an evening of pleasure. A man's mind, he insisted, had to be free of worry and of such heavy and disconcerting thoughts if he was to enjoy himself to the full. Accordingly, Donlin devised his own credit system. It meant added work for his bartenders, but it paid off handsomely.

When a customer was served a drink he scribbled his name on a tab which the bartender picked up and dropped into a box behind the bar. These tabs were carefully sorted out after hours and charged in a huge ledger, the biggest thing in books that anyone had ever seen. A whole page was allotted each customer.

On payday the cowboys came directly to Donlin's for settlement. Each man thumbed through the ledger which had been placed upon the bar, found his own page, glanced at the amount due, tore out the page and handed it to Donlin together with the amount owed. Donlin compared the totals, put the money into the tab box and returned the ledger sheet to the payee, who tore it to bits and tossed them away, hitched up his pants and accepted a generous drink on the house. The ceremony over, the cowboy moved away so that someone else could get to the ledger.

There was no complaints and everyone was delighted with the system. The fact that Donlin's customers drank more and spent more than they would have done under a strictly cash system was not the all-important thing—that is, to them. They felt that they were indebted to him for being able to enjoy themselves without worrying about money. Accordingly, on payday they showed their appreciation. Every account was settled.

By midnight the cowboys were usually broke again, after trying to buck the poker or faro games. Donlin's dealers were experts and, since they worked on a percentage basis, they corraled every loose dollar that was carried into the place. New ledger sheets were hastily prepared and the tab pads and pencils laid out.

Except for such brief interludes as roundup time, when the entire personnel of each outfit was pressed into service to help round up and prepare the saleable cattle for the eastward trek to the cattle markets and stockyards, or at branding time when the brands were checked over and renewed and newly acquired cattle branded, Donlin's did a consistent business. There were enough ranches within easy riding distance of town to give him a steady nightly trade, and week-ends, when everyone went to town, his place was packed.

McCloud had more than a dozen assorted cafés and saloons, but most of them eyed Donlin's crowded premises with the eye of envy, and morosely counted their meagre receipts. Donlin's chief competitors were Dave Weber's "Palace of Joy" and Joe Slater's "Happy Hour Inn." But he didn't worry too much about what business they might take from him. Their trade was made up largely of transients and strangers who were attracted to their places by lurid posters of dancing girls in daring and abbreviated costumes.

Both Weber and Slater furnished the stagecoach drivers with handbills, facsimiles of their posters, and with other advertising matter, and instructed them to distribute the throwaways among their male passengers.

One of Slater's handbills read:

Happy Hour Inn
Genial
Joe Slater
presents
The World's Most Beautiful
GIRLS
Singing ... Dancing
See them ... hear them
Dance with them
Drink with them

• • • •

A beautiful girl for every man!
Come one, come all ... BUT COME EARLY!
For that night you'll never

> forget
> come to
> Happy Hour Inn

Weber went after trade in his own inimitable way. One of his choicest bits of advertising took this form:

> YOU can win a GIRL!
> • • • •
> Dave Weber's
> PALACE OF JOY
> offers you the thrill
> of a lifetime … play
> GIRL LOTTERY
> and win a real GIRL

The Palace of Joy and the Happy Hour Inn were located on opposite sides of the street. The rivalry between them was intense. Their women entertainers doubled as "pullers-in" and pursued prospective customers up and down the street, and often across the street. Each group regarded their side of the street as sacred, and when one of the warring factions followed a prospect into alien territory, it was a signal for all hands to pile on. It was a common sight to see the street full of screaming, wrestling, gouging, hair-pulling women in tights.

Despite Donlin's refusal to employ women in his café, his patrons continued to crowd his place as if they had never heard of his competitors'. It was discouraging to his rivals, but they held on doggedly.

They strove mightily to win the confidence and friendship of the ranchers, but it was wasted effort, for the latter had long since discovered that Donlin was a confidant who understood their problems and that he could give advice and financial assistance with equal grace and facility.

In order to avoid publicity or embarrassment to the borrower, Donlin always insisted upon secrecy for his transactions. He always refused point-blank to accept anything for making a loan, but somehow his objections were always overridden by the borrower, who finally "forced" Donlin to accept a piece of property as collateral. Additional loans, as always made secretly, and never divulged to anyone, enlarged Donlin's holdings to such a point that soon he owned more than fifty per cent of the ranches between Fargo and Tonopah.

Every now and then his competitors got together, pooled their ready cash, and asked Donlin to put a price on his place, but he simply laughed at them, offered them a drink which they coldly refused and sent them on their way. He had a good thing and he knew it; and what was more, he proposed to hold on to it.

Tonight Donlin's was crowded as never before. It was payday and an in-between period, with little more to occupy the cowboys than their routine duties; hence, aside from a few who had remained at home to keep a weather eye on things, the men had ridden off to town for a spot of relaxation.

Tobacco smoke hung over the place like a limp, inert, overstuffed cloud. The strong smell of stale beer and spilt beer, of hops and malt and ale, thickened the air to the point of suffocation, but no one appeared to notice it, much less be bothered by it.

Donlin was standing near the open door when a tall, lithe, blond man sauntered inside. Donlin studied the newcomer carefully, noticing the brace of heavy Colts which hung low against his lean, muscular thighs. In one brief glance, Donlin had critically appraised the newcomer, and he nodded to himself. The man's guns, the way he walked, the manner in which he carried himself—the recognizable signs were all too obvious. The mark of the gun-master was on him. Donlin was not deceived by the boyishness of his friendly grin, nor the innocent gaze of his blue eyes. Doran glanced at Donlin as he strolled past him and halted presently at the near end of the bar. Donlin turned slowly, plodded after him and stopped beside him.

"Howdy," Donlin said.

Doran looked up. "Howdy," he said briefly. He rested his arms on the edge of the bar.

"Stranger here, ain't yuh?"

Dan avoided the question and called for a whiskey in a tone so docile that it seemed impossible for it to carry over the din. But the barkeep, four or five yards down the line, looked up instantly.

"Comin' up," he said.

Donlin nodded gently to himself. Killers sometimes had voices like that, as soft and drawling as a cat's purr, but invariably commanding instant and respectful attention.

"Here y'are," the barman said dully, and placed an uncorked bottle in front of Doran. He followed it almost immediately with a glass. "Help yourself, stranger."

Dan poured himself a drink, downed it, put down the glass and made a wry face.

"Wow!" he sputtered.

Donlin looked at him sharply. "S'matter?" he demanded. "Somethin' wrong?"

Doran's lips thinned. "No," he replied, coughing, "not a thing 'cept that I've just swallered a glass full of poison." He turned his head and spat across the floor. "Doggone if that ain't the rarin'est stuff I've ever put down my gullet. Say, who owns this joint?"

Donlin laughed softly. "Reckon I might's well own up," he replied. "I do. Why d' yuh ask?"

Doran's scowl was that of a schoolboy confronted with an impossible sum. "Why?" he echoed. "I can't understand how you can sell that kind of coyote sweat more than one time to a customer."

Donlin leaned over the bar. "It's agreeable to meet a good judge o' liquor. Mike," he called, "trot out a bottle o' my own stuff."

The bartender trudged away. He returned a minute later and placed another bottle in front of Doran, picked up the first bottle and carried it off. Donlin reached over and uncorked the fresh bottle and pushed it closer to Dan.

"Try that, mister," he suggested.

Doran looked at the bottle, up at Donlin, then down again at the bottle.

"Don't know as I ought," he said doubtfully. "This stuff might be even worse'n the other. Nope—that just ain't possible."

Donlin grinned amiably. "I don't think so," he replied. "I've been drinkin' this brand fer more'n a month an' I'm still around."

Dan pondered for a moment. "Well," he said finally, "all right then. It can't do any more'n kill me, can it?"

Donlin shook his head. "Nope," he said gravely. "That's the worst it kin do."

Dan filled his glass a second time and raised it to his lips. "Here's to good horses and bad hombres."

He drained the glass, then stiffened as he felt a gun suddenly jammed hard against his spine.

"Put it down," a cold voice commanded, "an' turn around."

The glass came down and rested on the bar. Doran counted three slowly and then turned. The gaping muzzle of a big Colt yawned at him. Behind the gun stood Foster, big and scowling. His two pals were a step behind him, their thumbs hooked in their belts. Doran saw the startled faces all around him. Card players forgot their cards and stood up so that they might see better. Dan noticed too that the saloon was suddenly hushed.

"So yuh wouldn't play smart an' get outa here while yuh had the chance?" Foster demanded. "Wa-all, mebbe now yuh'll almighty wish yuh had. Head for the door, mister—and mind yuh, no tricks."

Doran glanced at Donlin. "Keep out of this, Donlin," Foster warned him. "This ain't none o' yore party."

Donlin flushed and looked away. He stared down at the bar as if it were the most absorbing thing he had ever seen.

No help was coming from his direction. Doran shrugged good-naturedly. "Here I come," he said submissively.

Foster backed up to let him pass. "Come slow and easy," he directed, waving his gun.

Dan grunted, hitched up his pants and sauntered up to Foster. When he had reached the burly man's side, he pivoted suddenly and swiftly to drive his right fist into Foster's face. The blow landed with a solid thump on Foster's heavy jaw.

Foster floundered back and, after nearly falling when his legs buckled under him, managed to right himself with the aid of a nearby table. He shoved himself upright and leveled his gun.

A Colt roared angrily, the report racketing from the saloon walls with sudden thunder. It fired twice more—three snap-shots blasting loose within an eye's wink.

Blue smoke curled from the muzzle of Dan Doran's guns. Foster was oddly bent, his right arm limp. He swayed a little on widespread legs, and stared down at his own gun lying on the floor at his feet. His bleary eyes widened. The gun's barrel was twisted as if some giant hand had seized and bent it.

Foster raised his head slowly, almost cautiously. His eyes were glassy. He felt of his right arm gingerly, and when he found it sound and undamaged, he seemed unable to believe it. A tiny rivulet of bright red blood surged out of his mouth and ran down his chin; there was, too, a deepening red welt on his jaw. He coughed once and, making a face, spat out a tooth and stared at it in apparent fascination. He was like a man surveying and appraising a hurricane's unexpected havoc. He straightened up presently, stared at Doran for a moment, then looked around him, his eyes moving slowly in their sockets.

One of his friends lay back against the bar, his right arm hanging limply at his side. Blood ran down his fingers and dripped gently on the floor, forming a tiny pool within an inch of the gun that lay at his feet. The third man, white-faced and dazed, appeared rooted to the floor. His arms were half raised, stiffened and held fast by fear and indecision.

"All right, Foster," Doran said evenly. Foster turned toward him mechanically as though attracted by the sound of a voice rather than by the speaker himself. "Get this, mister—and get it right. Next time I won't shoot yore gun outa your hand. I'll blast yuh clear outa yore boots. Savvy? That's a promise, so keep thinkin' on it. Now take a stroll outa here."

Foster squared his shoulders, turned and lumbered out of the saloon. The man with the shattered arm straightened up. He stared at Doran for a moment, then lowered his eyes to his gun on the floor. He frowned, bent down and groped for the gun with his left hand. Doran whirled and kicked it away. It skidded across the floor and disappeared from sight among the crowded tables.

"Get outa here," Dan said soberly.

The man grunted, turned and plodded out, leaving a trail of blood on the floor. The third man lowered his arms, and backed toward the door. Midway he wheeled and bolted out. A wave of whispers swept through the crowded saloon, which had been so deathly still.

Doran holstered his guns and shifted them a bit, dug in his pocket and produced a coin and tossed it on the bar. He settled his hat more securely and sauntered toward the door. Just as he reached it a man arose from a table, stepped forward quickly and halted in front of him. Dan eyed him sharply. His thumbs hooked themselves in his gunbelt.

"I beg your pardon," the man said pleasantly. Doran ran his eyes over him. His speech was that of a city man, his tailor-made, well-fitting clothes definitely not of the region. "I'd like to talk with you."

"Go ahead."

"My office is only two doors from here," the man continued. "We can talk there in privacy, if you're willing."

"Who are you?"

The man smiled lightly. His parted lips revealed white, even teeth.

"I'm John Sears," he answered simply; then he added, "the county attorney."

Doran's eyebrows arched.

"Oh, yes? Aimin' to lock me up for defending myself against them three critters?" he asked.

"No," Sears replied. "I'm the prosecutor, my friend, not the sheriff."

"Oh."

"Furthermore," Sears continued, "I watched the whole play and you handled it—and them—magnificently. No one's going to arrest you, I promise you."

Dan relaxed. He'd been alert for more trouble, but it didn't look as if any were coming from Sears' direction.

"Thanks. You had me kind of worried there for a minute. What's on your mind?"

"Suppose we wait until we get to my office," Sears countered.

"S'all right with me," Doran said. "Lead the way. I'll kinda bring up the rear."

CHAPTER FIVE

AN OFFER AND AN
ACCEPTANCE

Sears' office occupied the upper floor of a narrow two-story building. "County Attorney" was neatly printed on the glass panel of his office door in modest, inch-high letters. Sears unlocked the door and threw it open, motioned to Dan to wait and strode inside. Doran heard him strike a match, then a second one. Presently a bright light flamed in a lamp on a squat, flat-topped desk in the middle of the room.

"Come in," Sears called.

Dan sauntered inside. While Sears fussed with the lamp, turning down the light and raising it, lowering it and turning it up again until the wick-flame satisfied him, Doran looked around.

The office was small, not more than fifteen feet square; and it was scrupulously clean.

On the far side of the room was a single window opening on the street. Just beyond was a sturdy wooden clothes-closet. In a corner, opposite the window, were two small filing cabinets. There were labels on both of them. One of them read, "McCloud—Official Papers"; the other was marked, "Sears—Personal."

An armchair stood behind the desk, while four hard, straight-backed chairs of matching wood were grouped around it.

"Nothin' on the desk," Doran muttered to himself. "This Sears is a smart one, all right. Don't leave anythin' out for a nosy feller like me to get a look at. I'd shore like to see what he's got in that there 'Personal' file. Bet I could find some mighty interestin' readin' matter in there."

Sears straightened up.

"Sit down, man," he said over his shoulder. "Sit down."

Dan closed the door behind him. He chose the chair nearest the desk and sat down and looked around again. Sears trudged to the closet and hung up his hat, came back to the desk and sat down. Doran swung around in his chair. Their eyes met. For a brief moment they studied each other, in critical appraisal.

"He ain't a bad-looking galoot," Dan mused to himself, "and he acts like he knows it. He's smooth and cute and smart. If he'd only quit smilin' all the time—anybody can tell it's put on. And them thin lips of his—unless I read the sign wrong, he's hard inside and ornery as hell when somebody crosses him. Take away all that fancy-dude smoothness and he'd be about as charmin' and polite as a mountain cat."

Sears was the first to look away, occupying himself with an almost invisible speck of dust on his coat lapel, which he brushed carefully off before he looked up again.

"I don't believe I caught your name," Sears began presently.

"No? I don't believe I mentioned it," Dan said. He grinned. "It's Doran."

"Thank you. Would you mind telling me what brings you to McCloud?"

"Oh, I don't know. Just got on my horse and come. That's all."

"I see." If Sears was skeptical, he kept it out of his voice.

"Know of some job around here I might speak up for?" Doran asked.

Sears considered for a moment. "Well," he said presently, "you might apply at the railroad camp near Moon Pass. They might have something for you."

Dan Doran frowned slightly. If Sears' remark about the railroad was a baited hook, he wasn't going to rise to it.

"Thanks," he said. He got to his feet and hitched up his belt, nodded to Sears and turned toward the door. "So long, mister. I'm no railroad man..."

"Just a minute, Doran," Sears said.

Doran halted, his hand on the door knob, and looked back over his shoulder.

"Yes?"

"Sit down, won't you?"

Dan watched him from behind sleepy lids. He shrugged his shoulders and sat down again.

"I meant no offense," Sears said smoothly. "I was merely trying to be helpful. However, since you don't appear to want any part of railroading, perhaps I can think of something else—something more in keeping with your talents."

"Go on talkin', mister," said Dan, without much interest.

Sears looked away. He frowned in thought as though he were debating something within himself. Then, after a moment, evidently having arrived at a decision, he raised his eyes again.

"Doran—" he began, and paused. "Doran, I want you to forget for a minute that I am an officer of the law. Just pretend that—well, that we're both common citizens. Understand? Now then, are you—that is, are you wanted anywhere?"

Doran eased back in his chair, and brought his fingertips together beneath his chin. "What's that got to do with me gettin' a job?" he wanted to know.

"Nothing—not a thing," Sears said quickly. "This is off the record, you know."

Dan held his big body in its relaxed position. Behind his sleepy lids, the blue eyes flickered slightly. He permitted the smallest smile to hover around the edges of his mouth. "I might be on the dodge. I might, at that."

"I see. And what might you have done?" Sears fenced.

"I might have killed a feller, mebbe—a dirty yeller coyote."

Sears straightened. "If you had, you couldn't afford to be too particular about a job, now could you?"

"No. Got to eat and live, y'know."

Sears nodded. "Exactly. Doran, it seems to me that a man who can handle his guns as capably as you can ought to be able to put that talent to profitable use."

"Yes. I suppose so. Know anybody I could brace for that kind of a job?"

Sears was silent again for a moment. "Perhaps," he said quietly. "You understand, of course, that a man who hires himself out as a gunman will be expected to—"

"Do the work of a gunman?" Doran demanded, with a knowing smile. There was an awkward moment of silence.

"You're prepared to do that sort of thing?"

"Why not?" Dan demanded. "Long's it means money, I'm willin' to try anything."

"All right," Sears said. "I think I can get you a job."

"You can?"

"Yes, I'm quite certain I can."

"Money talks my language, mister. So far you ain't said much."

The county attorney smiled.

"That is important, isn't it? Two hundred a month, I'd figure," Sears replied. "How does that sound?"

Doran grinned. "How?" he repeated. "I guess I could manage to keep my skin on my bones for two hundred bucks a month. I had a feelin' that sooner or later you'd say somethin' worth listenin' to. Where's this job and when can I get started on it?"

"You can start whenever you like."

"How about the first thing tomorrow mornin'—or am I rushin' you?"

Sears laughed softly. "You can start tonight," he answered, "if you like."

Dan climbed lazily to his feet. "I like. Just tell me where to go and what to do when I get there."

Sears pushed his chair back from the desk and got to his feet. "Ride north out of town tonight at eleven-thirty. About a mile out you'll find a band of men waiting. I'll get word to them, so they'll be expecting you. Foster will—"

Doran's eyebrows crawled slowly up his wind-tanned forehead, rested there quizzically a minute, then redescended.

"Foster, eh?"

"Yes. But you won't have any more trouble with him. I have an idea he'll be more than willing to forget all about tonight's unpleasantness. Anyway, he'll be in charge. He'll tell you what to do."

"Uh-huh."

"Remember—you're to join them at midnight. So you'd better allow yourself good time."

"Don't worry—I won't keep 'em waitin'."

Doran pushed his chair aside and ambled to the door. He opened it, turned in the doorway and looked back. He caught Sears' eye.

"Much obliged," he said.

Sears nodded. Dan went out.

It was exactly eleven-thirty when Doran left his hotel. He halted on the sidewalk and looked up at the sky. The glance was more mechanical than purposeful; it was a habit of days gone by. He sauntered out to the curb. Bess heard his step and looked up, recognized him and whinnied softly, pushed her head over the rail and rubbed her nose against his shoulder. He patted her sleek neck affectionately. He climbed into the saddle, wheeled her away from the rail and loped down the street, deserted now, except for a lone passerby who looked up casually when they came up to him, then turned away and plodded on.

Soon the nimble-footed mare was whirling over the moonlit range, carrying him swiftly to the rendezvous.

"Reckon my fun's about to begin," he murmured presently. "Wonder what kind of hell I'm in for tonight?"

He frowned and shifted again. Bess clattered over a stony stretch of ground. Her hoofs rang out sharply, breaking the stillness of the night. Then suddenly the mare jerked her head up, slackened her pace and whinnied softly. Doran looked up, tightening his grip on the reins. He caught a glimpse of a campfire up ahead, its bright light flickering through a screen of trees.

He stood in his stirrups so he could see better.

"Uh-huh," he grunted. "Reckon that's them all right."

He sank down into the saddle again, not noticing that Bess had halted, shifted his holsters and loosened the big Colts in their leather sheaths. He switched Bess' reins to his left hand, freeing his right. Instantly it dropped and came to a stop on his right thigh, inches away from the jutting butt of a ready Colt. He looked up presently and frowned.

"What are you waitin' for," he demanded.

Bess snorted and plodded away. Carefully she threaded her way through the shadowy trees; after a minute or two, they emerged and halted again on the fringe of a clearing.

The campfire blazed cheerfully in the middle of the clearing. There were eight or ten men ranged around it, of whom two or three were on their feet. The others squatted on their heels and warmed their hands over the fire. All of them looked up. Doran's right hand moved upward in a lazy salute.

"Howdy," he said.

The other horses were tethered in the shadows on the far side of the clearing. They twisted around and neighed. Bess responded with a high-pitched whinny.

"Foster around?" Doran asked.

A burly figure emerged from the far shadows and advanced upon the light. It was Foster. He trudged past the fire, glanced at the men grouped around it, turned his head and looked sharply at Doran, still sitting patiently astride the mare. Foster halted suddenly, turned and plodded back to the fire. Some of the men got up; the others merely looked at him.

"All right," he said gruffly. "Get your horses."

Dan noticed an almost guttural thickness in his voice. He grinned. He knew what had caused the impediment in Foster's speech and flexed the fingers of his right hand.

The rest of them climbed to their feet and moved with unhurried steps toward their waiting horses. Foster strode back to Doran.

"I'm in charge tonight, mister—an' I give all the orders," he said curtly. "That clear?"

"Reckon so. That's what I been told."

Foster grunted. "All right, then. This is a raidin' party. We're aimin' to run off some Bar-M stock. Stick close to me an' do what I tell yuh. And do it *when* I tell yuh!"

Doran nodded. The Bar-M? That was Ben Miller's outfit. He was thankful for the shadows that prevented Foster from noticing the expression on his face. Foster turned and strode away. The other men were mounted now and waiting. One of them came forward, leading Foster's horse by the bridle. Foster reached for the reins and jerked his horse to a halt, got a grip on the saddle horn and swung himself up. He wheeled his mount.

"All right?" he demanded. "Yuh all set? Doran, c'mon; yuh're ridin' side o' me. The rest fall in behind us in two's. Let's go!"

CHAPTER SIX
MURDER BY MOONLIGHT

THE rhythmic drum-roll of pounding hoofs broke the stillness of the night. Doran, holding his fleet and impatient
mare down to an even pace, gave Foster an occasional side-long,
curious glance; but the burly man, sullen and tight-lipped, stared
straight ahead. Dan craned over his shoulder at the shadowy
troop of men strung out behind him. There was no sound from
any of them, nothing but the measured clatter of their horses'
hoofs.

But now, in the rear rank, a horse stumbled and fell. His rider
was taken completely by surprise. He was jolted out of his saddle.
He sailed over his horse's head and struck the ground with a
resounding, teeth-rattling thud. The horse scrambled to his feet
and clattered away after the others.

Another horseman, twisting around in his saddle, looked
back and saw the onrushing riderless horse careening toward
him. He pulled up, wheeled his mount out of line and waited
until the plunging animal came abreast of him; then he reached
for the reins and jerked him to an abrupt halt. He led the panting
horse back to where his rider was dragging himself up from the
ground, and tossed him the reins. The man cursed and vented
his outraged feelings upon his horse, kicking him viciously. The
animal cried out and backed away; he reared up on his hind legs
and lashed out wildly with his fore hoofs.

Foster came riding down the line.

"What'n hell's the matter with yuh, yuh damn fool?" he snarled. "Wanna wake up the hull county so's everybody'll know what we're doin'? If yuh'd quit dreamin' 'bout that red-headed tramp back at Slater's place an' keep yore mind on what yuh're bein' paid tuh do, this wouldn't 've happened. Better smarten up, mister—y'hear? I'm gettin' plumb fed up with you. Now get back aboard that critter an' watch where yuh're goin'. We got things tuh do, an' time's a-wastin'."

Foster wheeled and cantered up to the head of the troop.

"Let's go!" he snapped over his shoulder.

The cavalcade moved off again. For a time they rode in silence; then, without warning, Foster swung his horse off the trail he had been following and piloted him onto grassy terrain. The others, watchful and alert now, followed in his steps. The wisdom of his move was at once apparent. The grass muffled the sharp clatter of pounding hoofs; deadened the echoing, metallic ring of iron-shod feet on stone and shale.

Foster suddenly spurred his mount. The animal leaped forward and raced away. Bess flashed after him, easily overtook him and ranged herself alongside of him again. She threw up her head and snorted, indicating her contempt of him and his speed. The rest of the men, not to be outdone or outdistanced, lashed their horses and managed to close up the gap between the two. men in front of them and themselves.

The party again resumed its even pace, but Bess was not content. She was aroused now and determined to show Foster's horse something about pace-setting. She suddenly bolted away. Doran fought desperately to check her, but the mare was aflame. For a minute—a minute that seemed an eternity—there was a breathless struggle for supremacy with the high-spirited, fleet-footed mare fighting furiously for her head and determined to run—and Doran, cool, collected and strong-armed and equally determined to hold her down.

Bess' bid for freedom was short-lived. Dan had "broken" her once—he proceeded to prove to her that he was still her master.

He snapped the reins back viciously. Snorting, snarling and frothing, the mare jerked to a halt, whirled like a dervish, first this way, then that way, striving with might and main to rid herself of the iron bit that cut deep into her mouth and threatened to choke her. She gave a sudden heave and a vicious, teeth-rattling lurch, reared up and side-stepped and whirled around again—but to no avail. Doran kept his seat and refused to relax his grip on the reins. Panting and heaving, Bess finally capitulated. Head bowed, she stood for a moment on widespread, quivering legs, fighting for her breath. She whinnied softly—a sign of complete surrender—and Doran wheeled her back into line.

Again the party went on. The swift-striding horses, running shoulder to shoulder, swept over the darkened, shadow-drenched turf, swung northward when Foster did, followed him into a grove of tall cottonwood trees and slid to an abrupt, saddle-creaking stop when he suddenly pulled up. Horses and men crowded around him. The men peered out from beneath the far-spreading branches of the trees. A hundred yards ahead of them, dark, hunched figures that experienced eyes soon recognized as cattle huddled against one another, milled aimlessly about and lowed. It was Miller's herd. There was no immediate or visible sign of the cowboys whose duty it was to guard the herd. Doran glanced at Foster. Despite the darkness that made everyone's face a featureless, indistinguishable blur, he thought he detected a grin on the burly man's face. It was evident that this raid was going to prove easier than expected. Miller had been caught off guard.

"Awright," Foster said crisply. "Yuh all know what tuh do, don'tcha?"

There was a chorus of muttered "Shores."

"When we get close tuh th' cattle, spread out," Foster went on. "We wanna see if we can't trap 'em between us an' drive 'em inter the river. Get th' idea? Awright. Now get yore guns out. You, too—Doran. You pack two o' them, don'tcha? Wa-al—let's see if yuh kin make 'em do the work o' two men. Everybody set? Then c'com!"

Foster drove his spurs into his horse's flanks. The animal cried out protestingly and bounded away. The others raced after him. Doran found himself hemmed in by shadowy, plunging horses.

"Shoot!" Foster cried.

Every gun in the band flamed. Doran's big Colts added to the din. Man-made thunder broke over the darkened range and rocked the earth, and gunfire blasted the blue skies. Whirling, wiry horses' legs swept the raiders onto the fringe of the huddling cattle. Volley after volley roared over their heads. The steers awoke to their danger, swung around in terror and piled into one another in a frantic effort to escape the onrushing horsemen. The result was not the expected stampede and the utter rout they had hoped for; it was instead chaotic confusion, with fear-maddened steers wheeling and scampering this way and that but with none of them getting anywhere. Then from out of the darkness behind them came an ominous clatter of galloping hoofs. It was Miller's Bar-M men. Too late the raiders realized that their plan had boomeranged—they were caught in their own trap. Too late, too, they tried to wheel their horses to face the new menace, but there was no turning now. They were completely hemmed in.

A blast of lead screamed into the ranks of the tightly packed raiders. A man cried out and fell forward against his horse's neck; the animal was hit too. He fell, crashing into another horse. Both went down in a tangle of threshing legs. Their riders managed to fight their way to their feet, but another outburst of gunfire wafted them away. In the confusion their own horses trampled them underfoot.

Another horse was badly wounded and toppled over. His rider jumped clear of him, wheeled and lunged desperately for a mate's saddle horn, but he missed and fell heavily. He staggered to his feet again and looked around frantically for an avenue of escape. A wave of cattle rolled over him and swept him out of sight.

Two horses reared up in fright when they were confronted by a solid wall of advancing steers. They crashed over backwards, crushing their riders beneath them. One horse tried to rise, but he was snowed under. His mate screamed once or twice; then the cattle billowed over him and he was silenced.

It was a rout—a complete and disastrous rout of the raiders. Of those who were still alive and who sought to stay alive, escape demanded the utmost, if not the impossible—survival in that swirling, engulfing current of milling cattle, then a successful coping with Miller's men who barred the rear, the path that led to the open range.

Dan Doran had survived thus far. He realized that he could not hope to survive much longer in that ever-surging sea of steers. At most it was only a matter of minutes before both he and Bess would be trampled into the dust. The pressure was increasing steadily, like a mounting storm. He would have to make a break for it through that only movable barrier—the Bar-M men.

He tightened his grip on the reins. He could feel the mare trembling under him. A careening steer skidded into her, and she screamed in terror and backed away, reared up and lashed out blindly with her fore hoofs. She cleared a path for herself, whirled like a cat and bounded away, only to collide heavily with another horse—Foster's. Both animals stumbled awkwardly and almost went down, but somehow they managed to steady themselves and bolted away again. Foster had evidently sensed what Doran proposed to do, for he quickly pulled up alongside of him. Instead of the obvious—instead of swerving away from the waiting Bar-M men and making a desperate run for freedom, they plunged full tilt into them.

The value of a surprise attack was never more clearly demonstrated. The cowboys moved forward to stop them, but the movement was individual, hesitant and lacking in damming power. Too late they resorted to the use of their guns to halt them—for by then the two fear-maddened horses were upon them. There was a sudden outburst of gunfire, close up, point-blank firing from Miller's men, then the terrific, stunning impact of a head-on collision.

Men and horses were brushed aside like vagrant leaves in the path of a sudden, droning wind. Others were simply bowled over by the viciousness of the charge. It lasted but a bare half-minute, and when it was over Foster and Doran had broken through and were thundering away, headed for the open range. A volley of shots, hastily and inaccurately fired, followed them. Men shouted angrily, and pursuing horses pounded after them madly. Foster turned in his saddle and emptied his gun into the ranks of the Bar-M men, who replied with a withering, spiteful blast of their own.

A bullet blazed a fiery trail across Doran's cheek. Another tore into his left shoulder.

He fell forward against Bess' neck, huddled there for a moment and finally forced himself upright again. The effort left him strangely weak and limp. Then, to cap it all, Bess stumbled over a half buried rock and pulled up, hobbling painfully.

Doran summoned his fast-ebbing strength. He shot a quick glance over his left shoulder. The Bar-M men, sensing victory, were closing in on them rapidly. Dan looked quickly at Foster, and realized with a sinking sensation that he could expect no help from him; he had emptied his gun and there was no time now in which to reload. The issue was squarely up to him—Doran.

He lifted one Colt. He had never noticed how heavy it was before. Strange, he told himself, that he should notice it now for the first time. His fingers tightened around the butt. He shifted it a bit. He would fire low, at the horses' legs. Perhaps that would do the trick. Perhaps if he shot down a few of them it would halt Miller's riders, or at least delay them just long enough for Foster and himself to get away.

He pressed his lips together and stifled a groan that arose in his throat. Slowly, painfully, laboriously, he raised his gun. Foster's horse veered sharply away from a boulder, misjudged the distance and whirled dangerously close to Bess, bumping her awkwardly as he pounded past her. Dan's arm was jolted. The big Colt roared suddenly, unexpectedly. He stared with unseeing, dimming eyes, failing to see a man in the front rank of the Bar-M riders sag and topple out of his saddle. He did not see the Bar-M men pull up, dismount hastily and scamper back to their fallen comrade.

His eyes closed gently. His gun slipped out of his numbed fingers. He felt no pain now—nothing but a curious drowsiness and an overpowering desire to sleep. He sighed wearily, relaxed and slid forward a second time against Bess' neck. The mare hobbled away. After she had gone a few hundred yards she turned into a grove of trees. No one noticed which way she went; it was evident from the fact that no one pursued her. Those who had pursued her before were now bent over a limp, huddled figure in the grass. After a while Bess halted. Shadows danced over her and around her, but she disregarded them.

Her leg bothered her, hampered her. She rubbed her nose against her leg. She whinnied softly, but there was no affectionate, familiar hand to pat her sleek neck or comfort her. Presently Doran slid out of the saddle. He landed on his shoulder, rolled over on his face and lay still. The mare turned slowly, stiff-leggedly, favoring her injured leg, and looked down at him. She nudged him, but there was no response.

A mile away Foster pulled up and wheeled his panting horse. He looked back, listened intently for a minute and frowned.

There was no sound, no echoing clatter or muffled pounding of a horse's hoofs. He jerked the reins sharply, wheeled his mount again and galloped away into the night.

The sky was curiously vacant now. The bright stars and the moon had gone. Far away, beyond the hills that were now nothing but a solid, indistinguishable mass of shadowy blackness, a faint and feathery glow of light suddenly appeared in the sky. A light breeze droned over the range. It rustled through the lush grass, whistled through the trees and raced away. Now the distant hills began to take on form. They cast off the shadowy veil of night and bared their rugged outlines.

Far away, Foster glanced skyward. It would soon be dawn, he told himself. He permitted his horse to slow down, turned in the saddle and looked back and listened. Still there was no sound of hoofs. He shrugged his broad shoulders, settled himself in the saddle again and loped away.

CHAPTER SEVEN
A CHARGE OF MURDER

T HERE was a strained, oppressive silence in John Sears' office—the kind of sudden, smoldering silence that usually follows an angry outburst and a heated exchange of words. The silence was a temporary respite, a momentary "breather," for there was more to be said on both sides and the saying was about to begin again. There were two participants, Ann Miller, the daughter of the Bar-M owner, and John Sears, in his official capacity as county attorney. They faced each other quietly, the one unafraid, scornful, demanding and insistent; the other cold, tight-lipped and unmoved.

There was a third person present—pudgy, sweaty, red-faced Sheriff Ike Boone—but neither Ann nor Sears paid much attention to the lawman.

"Well, Mr. Sears?" Ann demanded. "What do you propose to do about this man—this Doran?"

The county attorney looked up. Their eyes met and clashed.

"Ann..."

"Miss Miller," she snapped, interrupting him.

Sears smiled lightly.

"Forgive me," he said gravely, almost gently. "I forgot for the moment that you are now a grown lady rather than the little girl—"

"Who disliked and distrusted you the very first time she saw you," she interrupted again, "and who has never changed her opinion of you since."

Sears' eyes glinted. His face grew thinner, harder.

"If you will permit me to continue," he said coldly, and paused.

"Shore, Ann," Sheriff Boone said. "Yuh might's well hear 'im out. Buttin' in on him all the time ain't gonna get yuh nowheres, y'know."

Both turned as one and gave him a withering glance. Boone flushed, turned his head slightly and coughed behind a pudgy hand.

"Miss Miller," Sears began again presently, "to sum things up, you tell me that your father was killed last night by a raider who rode a white horse. You insist that I issue a warrant for the arrest of this man. From your very meagre description—and certainly, in all fairness, you must admit that it is very meagre, almost negligible—I have identified him as a man who introduced himself to me only last night and who told me his name was Doran. I have told you, too, that in our very brief conversation, which was of a purely general nature, he informed me that he had come to McCloud in search of work and that he had been advised to apply at the railroad camp."

"Well?" Ann demanded impatiently.

Sears cleared his throat.

"To continue," he went on shortly, "doesn't it seem odd to you that a man who was interested in throwing in his lot with the railroad outfit would participate in an attack upon a cattleman who was known to be sympathetic to the cause of his prospective employers? Then, too—and I think you will agree that this is important—Doran and Foster, whom you also accuse of having been a member of this same raiding party, engaged in a fight last night. I witnessed it, and I assure you it was a hard-fought, bitter affair. Certainly the two oppents would hardly have joined forces immediately after and taken part in a raid such as the one which you report."

Boone grunted, but this time neither of them appeared to notice it or him. Their attention was too completely centered upon each other to permit distraction.

"Therefore, Miss Miller," Sears went on in a calm and unruffled tone, "after considering the evidence submitted, or rather your allegations, I regret to say that I find them at variance with common sense."

A frown darkened Ann Miller's face.

"Indeed. Then you refuse to do anything to help bring this man to justice?" she demanded.

"Not at all," Sears said quickly. "Not at all. I simply decline to make myself and my office a party to prejudice. Certainly you must realize that your father's refusal to join his brother ranchers in presenting a solid front against the unwarranted and uncalled for intrusion of the railroad must have earned for him the undying animosity of certain people. Some of them may have decided to take drastic action against him. Who they might be would be pure conjecture on my part. Now, if I were to issue a warrant for the arrest of every man in and around McCloud who owns or rides a white horse, I'm afraid our jail facilities would prove completely inadequate."

"Uh-huh," Boone said. "Besides, it'd shore be overcrowded."

"Please—" Sears snapped.

"Huh? Oh—excuse me."

"Miss Miller," the county attorney continued, "I shall investigate this matter. I promise you that. Other than that, I'm afraid I can't do very much for you at this moment. In fact, all I can do now is express to you my deepest sympathy in your bereavement."

Ann's face was white. Tiny patches of crimson darted into her cheeks.

"Thank you," she said coldly, controlling herself. "Your sentiment is very touching and your desire to help rid McCloud of lawlessness is very enlightening. I shall make it a point to see that it reaches the ears of the poor, deluded fools who elected you to office. I'm sure they'll feel proud of themselves and of their choice. You not only fail in your duty to them, the very people you swore to defend, but you do everything to thwart justice. You aren't an ordinary criminal, John Sears—you're an archcriminal. You're responsible for my father's death—you and the contemptible Dorans you shield!"

"Now, Ann—" the sheriff began.

The girl whirled to face him.

"Don't you dare speak to me!" she cried angrily. "You—you miserable fool!"

Ike gulped.

"Doggone it, girl," he sputtered. "Yuh can't go 'round callin' folks names an'—"

But Ann was finished with him. She disregarded him now and turned toward John Sears for a parting shot.

"I'm going to see to it," she said coldly, "that your friend Doran pays for his crimes. I'll fight you just as my father did, and if you murder me as you did him, depend upon it, there'll be someone else to carry on the fight for us—until you receive the punishment due you."

She turned on her heel. Boone backed away hastily, as though he expected her to strike him. She strode to the door and flung it open and fled. The door banged loudly behind her. For a brief minute they heard her quick step on the stairs that led to the street. They heard the outer door open and slam; then she was gone.

"Wh-e-w," the sheriff muttered.

There was no answer or comment from Sears. He pushed his chair back from the desk, climbed to his feet and came slowly around the desk, brushed past Boone and paced the floor. The sheriff followed him with his eyes. Sears halted abruptly.

"Ike."

"Yeah?"

"If, as the girl claims, the Bar-M men did wound Doran, the chances are that he couldn't have gotten very far away from the scene of the attack, could he?"

Boone shrugged his shoulder.

"Dunno, John," he replied. "There ain't no way o' tellin' 'less yuh knowed how bad he was hit."

"I suppose not. Ike, I didn't tell you—I didn't get the chance to—but I hired Doran and sent him along with Foster and those other blundering fools."

"Uh-huh. I kinda figgered it was somethin' like that from the way yuh tried tuh squirm outa doin' anythin' 'bout this Doran feller."

Sears disregarded the sheriff's comment. He was thinking of something else—something more important.

"If Doran were wounded," he mused, "and if he happened to fall into the hands of—we-ll, let's say the Bar-M outfit, he might talk."

Ike grunted.

"He might—shore."

"Then we can't afford to chance it," Sears said determinedly. "We must prevent it."

"Prevent what?" Boone demanded. "His fallin' inter some-body's hands or his talkin'?"

"Obviously, both."

"H'm," the sheriff muttered. "Dunno 'bout the one—an' the on'y perm'nent way I ever knowed o' shuttin' a feller's mouth was tuh kill 'im."

Their eyes met. "Well?"

Boone eyed Sears curiously.

"Yuh're shore actin' free'n easy lately with other fellers' lives," he drawled. "Ain'tcha?"

The county attorney's face was grim and hard.

"When it means their lives or mine," he said curtly, "there isn't any alternative."

"S'ppose not."

"I want you to look for him, Ike," Sears said quietly.

The sheriff frowned darkly.

"I kinda figgered yuh was leadin' up tuh that, John," he said slowly. "S'ppose I find 'im an' get 'im tuh promise tuh keep his mouth shut? That satisfy yuh?"

Sears shook his head.

"No," he said firmly, "it won't. Doran's already done more than I dared hope in ridding us of Ben Miller. With the completion of the very first job he undertook in our behalf, his usefulness to us is at an end. Now, as long as he lives there'll always be the fear that he'll talk—that he'll get ambitious and try to cut into things—that he'll demand more and more of us. No, Ike, it won't do. We can't go on with that fear hanging over our heads."

"If he cashes in, that'll be the end of 'im an' of our worries, eh?" Boone mused.

"Yes."

Ike considered for a moment, then shrugged his shoulder.

"Awright," he said heavily, with a tone of finality. "If that's the way it's gotta be, reckon that's the way it'll be. Ain't no two ways 'bout it that I kin see."

Sears relaxed. A smile broke over his mouth. "Thank you, Ike. You're always so understanding and appreciative of our mutual problems and difficulties."

"Ain't I though?"

The sheriff hitched up his belt. He shifted his holster to his hip, straightened up, glanced at Sears and turned slowly toward the door.

"Oh—Ike."

The pudgy man halted and looked back over his shoulder.

"Yeah?"

"You'd better go alone."

Boone frowned.

"'Course I'm goin' alone," he snapped. "Yuh don't s'ppose I want 'ny witnesses tuh what I'm gonna hafta do—do yuh?"

Sears laughed softly.

"Hardly," he replied.

Boone snorted, snapped his hat brim down over his eyes and opened the door.

"See yuh later," he said, and sauntered out.

Bud Watkins had accompanied Ann into McCloud. Reluctantly he had tied up both of their horses at the hitching rail in front of the general store far down the street—reluctantly because he had wanted to go along with her to Sears' office. Ann, however, had ruled against it. Now, pacing the curb impatiently, he frowned as he scanned the length of the narrow sidewalk, looking eagerly for Ann's slim figure.

"Damn it," he said thickly. He spied an inoffensive pebble lying within range of his boot toe, glared at it, drew back his foot and kicked it across the gutter. "Why'n hell didn't I say, 'Nope, if I ain't goin' with yuh, yuh ain't goin' either'? That Sears is cute, an' from what I've been told about 'im I wouldn't trust the polecat far's I could throw 'im."

Once or twice he had hitched up his gun belt and squared his shoulders and, contrary to Ann's instructions, had started doggedly up the street toward the county attorney's office. But each time, reluctantly again of course, he had halted and turned slowly and retraced his steps.

Now he spied Ann. He strode swiftly up the street to meet her. A dozen feet away he sensed that all was not well. He halted directly in front of her and gripped her slender shoulders. She raised her eyes to his.

"Ann," he said quickly, "what's the matter?"

"Nothing."

He frowned and slowly lowered his hands.

"How'd yuh make out with Sears?" he asked.

She shook her head.

"I didn't," she said simply.

"Yuh mean tuh say that smilin' polecat wouldn't do anythin'?" he demanded.

"That's right, Bud."

"Why, the dirty dog!" he gritted through his teeth. His hand dropped swiftly and tightened around the butt of his gun. "I got a good mind tuh go up there an' give that ornery critter a taste o' somethin' he's had comin' to 'im fer a long time. Doggone it, Ann, why didn't yuh listen tuh me an' let me go along with yuh, huh?"

She smiled wanly.

"It wouldn't have done any good," she replied. "There would have been a fight, and we'd have been even worse off than we are now."

"Yeah, I s'ppose so," he admitted grudgingly; then his eyes gleamed. "On'y I'da had the satisfaction o' handin' him somethin' he wouldn'ta fergot in a hurry."

"Come on, Bud—let's go home."

He nodded mutely, took her by the arm and led her to the horses. He held a stirrup for her, helped her mount and handed her the reins. A horseman loped past them. Bud looked up. It was the sheriff. A frown darkened his face.

"There's another one I'm gonna tangle with some day," he said thickly; then he added in a lower tone, "The low-down coyote."

He turned away, untied his horse, vaulted into the saddle and wheeled him away from the rail.

"C'mon."

Together they rode out of McCloud.

CHAPTER EIGHT
BUD WATKINS
PAYS A DEBT

A s BUD and Ann neared the river, cool, brisk breezes raced forward to meet them, swirled around them and rustled the grass into protested wakefulness. The thick grass absorbed and cushioned the vibrant pounding of the horses' hoofs. They had settled down to a steady, loping gait when the breeze grew sharper and the horses, stung by the sudden chill, snorted and quickened their pace.

Bud glanced at Ann again.

"Pore kid," he muttered to himself. "She's shore takin' it hard. Why'n hell did a square-shooter like her old man hafta cash in instead of a hellion like that Sears? Or some other polecats that ain't done nobody a mite o' good? It don't make sense takin' the good an' leavin' the bad tuh do more bad."

He shifted himself a bit and resumed his mumbling.

"But that doggoned Doran galoot—" he continued with a trace of disappointment and bitterness in his undertone. He shook his head. "There's one feller I don't savvy nohow. I'm blamed if yuh kin ever tell 'bout anybody. I coulda bet my last chip on Doran. There was somethin' 'bout him that made yuh like 'im. But lookit what become of 'im? Heck—just 'n ord'nary gun-throwin' raider. I'd shore like tuh know how he come tuh tie up with that Foster an' his bunch."

Ann's horse suddenly darted away, and Bud cursed him under his breath, spurred his mount and finally overtook them and pulled up alongside of them. He glared at Ann's mount but forgot about him in another instant, for in the distance he saw a horseman whirl into view. He frowned, studied the rider through narrowed eyes, wondering who he was and what he was doing on Bar-M property. Then Bud pulled up suddenly. Ann's horse, taking his cue from the youth's mount, halted so abruptly that the girl was almost jolted out of her saddle. She looked quickly at Bud.

"What—what is it?" she gasped.

Bud studied the horseman for another moment before he answered.

"Look over there, Ann—toward that ridge on the right. See 'nything?"

Her eyes followed his pointing finger.

"Why, yes. It's a man."

"Uh-huh. He look f'miliar to yuh?"

Ann took another look.

"No," she said slowly. "I don't think so."

Bud frowned impatiently.

"Heck, Ann," he sputtered. "Don't tell me yuh don't rec'nize the sheriff when yuh see 'im. I'd know that critter any time an' anywheres."

Now, given a hint as to the man's identity, Ann studied him more carefully.

"Of course, Bud, it is the sheriff. But what is he doing out here on the Bar-M?"

The youth shook his head.

"Dunno yet," he replied, "but I aim tuh know pronto. We'd better get closer tuh the buzzard an' kinda keep 'n eye on 'im. Whatever he's up tuh, yuh kin bet yore last chip on it, it ain't fer anythin' good. C'mon."

The two horses dashed away. The sheriff had slowed his mount, and it was a simple matter for them to narrow the distance that separated them. Mechanically Bud loosened the gun in the holster that swung against his hip. It was a typical western mannerism—a "just in case" precaution. It was something that every cowboy learned early in life and never forgot.

Bud swung his horse close to Ann's.

"Ann!"

"Yes?"

"Keep ridin' straight ahead," he commanded. "Boone's turnin' north. I'm gonna foller 'im. I'll see yuh at the house afterwards. Watch out fer yoreself—y'hear?"

He jerked the reins sharply and swerved away.

"Bud!"

He twisted around in the saddle.

"Yeah?"

"Be careful!"

He grinned boyishly.

"Ain't I allus?"

He jabbed his horse with his spurs. The animal darted away. Bud fastened his eyes on Boone, then turned once for a quick, backward, reassuring glance in Ann's direction. He saw that she was following his instructions, turned and concentrated his attention on the sheriff. He followed the unsuspecting lawman for some time, and finally saw him pull up. Bud whirled his mount into a nearby thicket, and just in time, too, for the sheriff turned in his saddle and looked back. Presently, satisfied that the range was deserted and that he hadn't been seen, Boone dismounted.

There was a double row of cottonwood trees beyond the thicket, and Bud headed for it. Although the trees furnished him with a protective screen, he went forward cautiously. He had no wish to be detected now. He jerked to a halt when Boone appeared far ahead of him among the trees and backed his horse out of sight. He dismounted quickly and scrambled forward, froze in his tracks when he heard a horse whinny, turned slowly and looked back and seemed puzzled when he saw his horse busily and contentedly munching grass. Then a white horse suddenly jogged into view, midway between the two men. Bud took refuge behind a tree. He peeked out and saw the sheriff plodding toward the horse. Bud got a second look at the animal. There was something familiar about it.

"Doran's!" he muttered. "Wa-al, what d'yuh know!"

The sheriff circled the mare, looked sharply at her legs and hips, evidently searching for her owner's brand, scowled when he found none and picked up a twig and threw it at her. The animal shied away, wheeled and trotted off. But she halted presently, looked back over her shoulder and whinnied again.

"H'm," Bud muttered. "Doggone if she don't act like she was tryin' tuh say somethin'—mebbe like, 'C'mon, Mister—foller me'. Wish tuh hell that buzzard wasn't here so's I could take a look aroun'."

He forgot about the sheriff for a moment and eyed the mare carefully, trying to interpret her actions and wondering if she really were trying to say something. Then the pudgy Boone, gun in hand, came plodding across Bud's line of vision. He trudged up to the white horse. This time she made no attempt to avoid him or back away from him. Instead she whinnied softly. The sheriff gave her a sidelong glance, pushed past her and started into some brush just behind her, where he halted suddenly and stared hard.

His gun came up slowly as though he were about to shoot. He checked his arm and lowered his gun and pushed on again, farther into the brush, halted again presently and raised his gun a second time. He grunted loudly. His finger curled around the trigger when the blunt muzzle of another gun was shoved hard into the small of his back.

"Hold it!"

Boone stiffened.

"Awright—drop yore gun!"

The sheriff did not obey immediately. He gulped and swallowed and braced himself.

"Hey!" he sputtered. "Whoever yuh are—I'm th' sheriff—y'hear?"

Bud laughed coldly.

"I know it," he said curtly and scornfully, "so don't brag about it. Just do's yuh told an' drop yore gun."

This time Boone obeyed. Bud pushed him out of the way. Boone nearly fell into the brush, but he managed somehow to keep his feet and straightened up. Meanwhile Bud had bent swiftly, picked up the gun and hurled it away. He jabbed the sheriff with the muzzle of his gun just to remind him that he was still there and looked over Boone's shoulder. In a tiny clearing within a circle of brush lay a sprawled, motionless figure. It was Doran. He stirred slightly at that very moment, and Bud's eyes glinted.

He swung Boone around angrily.

"Why, yuh ornery polecat," he gritted. "That feller's alive, an' if I hadn'ta stopped yuh, yuh'da plugged 'im an' finished 'im off! Yuh're a fine lawman, awright. Doggone yore hide—I oughta let yuh have it right here an' now—right through that pot belly o' yourn!"

The sheriff's face whitened.

"Now—now, just a minute there, Watkins," he began. " 'Less I'm plumb mistaken, that there feller's the one Ann's accused o' killin' her ol' man. She was hollerin' fer Sears tuh do somethin' about this hombre, an' now when I find 'im, you throw down on me. I got a good mind tuh 'rrest yuh fer interferin' with th' law—yuh know that?"

Bud's lips thinned dangerously.

"If yuh think the idea's worth doin' somethin' about, I'll give yuh a chance tuh go get yore gun," he said coldly. "Then yuh kin try arrestin' me—if yuh got th' guts. Go 'head. I won't start blastin' the minute yuh turn aroun'.'"

But Boone made no attempt to move. He blinked and swallowed again.

"Doggone yuh, Watkins," he began.

"Shut up," the youth commanded. "Yuh're a yeller dog, Boone—with or without that tin badge o' yourn. Now get outta here an' stay outta here. If I catch yuh snoopin' aroun' th' Bar-M, I'll blast yore fat carcass all over the range. Understan'? Get goin'."

The sheriff flushed, circled him and plodded away. Bud followed him into the open, halted on the fringe of the range, watched him mount and saw him wheel his horse.

"I'll be seein' yuh sometime!" Boone yelled over his shoulder. "Mebbe yuh won't be so all-fired smart'n tough then!"

Bud's gun roared. A bullet jerked the sheriff's hat from his head. It sailed across the grass. Bud's gun flamed a second time, twice, three times more. The bullets tore into the hat and sent it spinning crazily. It finally slowed and collapsed on the grass. There was a murderous look on Boone's face. His lips moved, but indistinctly. He spurred his horse and galloped off toward town. Bud waited until he was out of sight; then he reloaded his gun and shoved it into his holster. He turned and trudged back to where the unconscious Doran lay sprawled out. Bud bent over him.

"H'm," he muttered presently. "Yuh shore got a honey of a hole through yore shoulder, mister. Good thing fer you that the blood's hardened 'round the hole an' plugged it up an' stopped the bleedin', otherwise yuh wouldn't be 'mong those present fer long. Reckon I won't monkey with yuh. The best thing I kin do is get yuh outta here an' pronto, an' then see 'bout fixin' yuh up."

He straightened up. The mare came toward him slowly and whinnied softly again.

"C'mere," Bud said.

Bess seemed to sense that the youth was a friend. She came closer without hesitation or fear and rubbed her nose against his shoulder. Bud patted her neck gently.

"That's a good girl," he said. He reached for the reins, backed the mare and brought her up close to the motionless Doran. "Now stan' still, Baby, so's we kin get yore boss up on yuh. He's hurt bad, and we gotta get 'im outa here—savvy?"

The mare seemed to understand and indicated it by a toss of her head. Bud grinned and patted her again; then he quickly bent over Doran and turned him over on his back. He pulled the unconscious man up on his feet, held him tightly for a moment and inched him closer to the mare; then, straining his muscles to the very limit, he managed somehow, miraculously in view of the fact that Doran was far bigger and heavier than he, and dead weight at the moment, to boost him up into the saddle. Carefully he lowered him against Bess' neck.

"Boy!" he panted finally. "That was somethin'. Now set still, Mister. I'm gonna rope yuh tuh yore saddle; then I won't hafta worry none 'bout yuh tumblin' out."

He turned away slowly, halted after he had taken a few steps and looked back. When he felt that Doran would be safe, he wheeled and raced away through the trees toward his own horse. He came galloping back astride him in another minute, slid to the ground beside the waiting mare and snatched a lariat from his saddle horn. Swiftly and securely he lashed Doran to the mare, then, finished, he stepped back, hands on his hips, and looked him over, circled him to make certain that he would not be jolted out of the saddle, nodded to himself and turned again to his own horse and mounted him.

Then he frowned as a puzzling thought came into his mind.

"Now why'n hell was Boone aimin' tuh kill off this feller?" he asked himself. "As a lawman, he shoulda been satisfied just tuh capture 'im. But here he was drawin' a bead on 'im. Funny—but I don't savvy it nohow."

Then another disturbing thought crowded Boone out of his mind.

"Hell, I gotta take this hombre somewheres. Can't just leave 'im out here. It's a safe bet I can't lug 'im inter M'Cloud fer Boone tuh finish off, an' I can't tote 'im up tuh the house either. Ann'd just about have my life if I was tuh try tuh do anything like that. Reckon the on'y place I kin take 'im to is that ol' shack down near the river. Nobody ever goes near it, so he oughta be safe there fer a while, leastways till he's able tuh hightail it away on his own."

He leaned out of the saddle and caught hold of the mare's bridle, straightened up and nudged his horse with his knees. Both horses wheeled.

"Easy, now," Bud cautioned them.

Slowly they made their way through the trees and emerged presently on the open range.

Bud gave Doran a final check, tested the rope and then settled back in his own saddle.

"Go 'head," he said.

Together the two horses plodded away.

CHAPTER NINE
AN UNINVITED GUEST

IT WAS late afternoon of the same day, and the slim figure of a girl who was Ann Miller sauntered slowly and aimlessly along the river bank. The breeze forced her to halt and turn up the collar of her jacket around her neck. Her hands dug deep into her pockets. She sighed wearily and looked up.

"It's—it's going to rain," she heard herself say in a small, hollow voice.

And rain it did—at first a light drizzle, followed almost instantly by a strong downpour. She plodded on up the bank.

Without shelter and without a horse, she was at the mercy of the elements. The rain began to come down in sheets, and a rumbling, rolling, echoing clap of thunder and lightning that seemed to rend the sky frightened her. She looked about her quickly.

Somewhere beyond her she spied a small structure. In the poor light she did not recognize it at once; it was only after a second, jagged streak of lightning lit up the sky that she was able to recognize it. It was small and dismal-looking, but at the moment it was more than she had dared hope for; it was a haven and it represented safety. Her father had had it built many years before. It was a sort of range storehouse in which branding-irons and other bits of equipment, most of them long since discarded in favor of newer tools, were kept. She buttoned her collar and dashed toward the shack. She stumbled once or twice, fell to her knees once, but she forced herself up again and went on until she finally reached the shack and burst in. In her excitement she failed to be surprised to find the door unlocked. Once inside, she turned quickly and slammed the door shut and sank back against it, breathless and bedraggled.

Then, as she regained her breath and composure, she suddenly became aware of someone else in the shack—someone who breathed deeply and laboriously. For a moment her heart pounded up into her throat and the icy hand of fear clutched her tightly. She brushed a stray strand of wet, straggly hair away from her eyes. On the far side of the shack was a crude, makeshift bunk. There was a small, upended box beside it; on the box was a basin of water and a lighted lamp with a wobbly base and a tilted and broken shade. Rays of light sifted through the gaps in the shade and curiously formed shadows capered and flitted over the ceiling and walls. On the bunk itself was a long, blanketed figure—a man.

Ann gasped. Fright at the sudden discovery gripped her. She turned, tempted to flee from the shack and to face the elements again. But weariness stayed her and forced her to bridle her fright.

"Who—who are you?" she asked in a nervous and unfamiliar voice.

There was no reply.

Her hand stole behind her, found the door knob and tightened around it. If the blanketed figure moved she would have whirled and burst out. She watched the man fearfully, as though she expected him to leap suddenly from the bunk. But there was no movement—not even the barest suggestion of a movement—beneath the blanket. She tried the door, turned the knob carefully and stealthily. It would never do, she told herself, to let him know, if he were playing possum, that she was preparing herself for an instant dash if it became necessary. Assured that the door would open without any difficulty, she felt relieved.

Minutes went by, but still nothing happened. Time gave her courage. She drew a deep breath and tiptoed across the floor toward the bunk. The floor creaked dismally beneath her. Half a dozen times she froze in her tracks, certain that he had moved, but each time when nothing happened, she grew just a bit bolder and took still another step forward. Then she reached the bunk and looked down.

The man was asleep. He was breathing deeply—too naturally to be feigning sleep. It gave her added courage, and she bent over him. There was a bloodstained piece of tape across one cheekbone. His right arm hung limply over the low side of the bunk, and his hand, open and relaxed, almost touched the floor. She studied his face for a moment. One look told her that she had never seen him before. He was young and blond, and from the length of him, a big man. She noticed too that he was a good-looking young man.

He stirred slightly. The blanket was drawn up over his left arm and shoulder, concealing them. When he moved them, even the barest bit, a grimace of pain swept over his face and his lips compressed. When the twinge abated he gave an involuntary sigh and seemed to relax. His lips moved, and she knew that he had mumbled something, but it was faintly uttered and indistinct. She drew closer. His lips moved again. She saw that they were parched and fever-dry.

"Water," he mumbled.

For a moment she did not move; then she turned and looked about her. There was a huge packing case against the opposite wall. On top of the case was a tin cup. She strode over and caught it up, retraced her steps and scooped up some water from the basin, bent over him again and managed to get a few drops into his mouth.

She put down the cup, pushed back the wet sleeve of her jacket and slipped her bare arm under his head and raised him a bit; then she lifted the cup to his lips. After a minute he seemed quite satisfied. She lowered him gently and withdrew her arm. He sighed and settled himself deeper in the bunk. She put down the cup again.

For another minute she stood over him, watching him, but he turned slowly, heavily, his face to the wall. She backed away, on tiptoe as before so as to avoid disturbing or awaking him. This time there was little or no creaking from the floor. There was a small window directly above the packing case, and she made her way over to it and looked out. The pane glistened under the deluge of swirling rain, but it was impossible to see through it.

The man stirred again, and she turned quickly, but there was no sound from him. Now the rain came down with a terrifying intensity. Somewhere in the distance she heard the deep-throated rumble of thunder, but it was only a threat and it subsided presently. Now the pounding rain on the roof sounded like racing cushioned feet coming closer and closer, like a wolf pack on the trail; then that too slackened shortly and faded away. Suddenly, she realized that she was cold. She looked about her quickly, searching eagerly for a stove, but there was none.

She unbuttoned her jacket and shook it. Raindrops spattered the floor. The man turned again, and the blanket slipped away from him toward the edge of the bunk. She frowned and bent over him again and tucked the blanket under him. Her hand brushed his face. It was smooth but hot and feverish. She shook her head. This business of caring for a sick man—a stranger at that—was more than she had bargained for.

She dug into her pocket and produced her handkerchief and dipped it into the basin, squeezed most of the water out of the tiny square of linen and gently bathed his face and brow; then she did the same to his wrists. Half a dozen times within the next thirty minutes she repeated the process. He was breathing much easier now, and she noted too that his face felt cooler to the touch. She forced some water into his mouth, then carried the cup and basin over to the packing case and put them down upon its broad surface, followed them with the lamp and moved the box away from the bunk. With the lamp shifted to the far side of the shack, the glare of light that broke through the shade was lessened.

She seated herself on the box. A sigh of weariness escaped her. She raised her head and listened again to the rain. It hadn't let up any as yet. After a time she arose and tiptoed to the window and peered out. She could see nothing—nothing but swirling, windblown rain. She retraced her steps to the box and sat down again. She turned her head and glanced at the sleeping man. She wondered who he was and what he was doing on Bar-M property—wondered, too, how long he had been there.

She puzzled over it for a time, until drowsiness crept over her and dulled her senses. Her eyes closed. She struggled for a minute to keep them open, to stay awake, but it was a weak, ineffectual, half-hearted effort on her part, and in the end she surrendered and accepted the soothing embrace of sleep. She dozed off. Her head came down slowly. She stirred once or twice, a momentary twitching of frayed nerves and tired muscles in a tired body. Presently she was still.

The bright morning sun forced its way into the shack through the small window on the far side of the structure. Warm, vibrant rays danced over the walls and flooded it with dazzling light. Ann awoke with a start. She looked about the shack quickly, dazed for a moment as a result of her sudden awakening and unable to understand where she was. She made a wry face and put her hand to her neck when she felt a sudden twinge there, and rubbed it gently. Presently the stiffness wore off. She was wide awake now. In that instant she remembered everything, particularly the man on the bunk, and she turned quickly and looked at him.

He was still asleep, and his face was still turned toward the wall.

Then as her eyes ranged over him she remembered what she had been puzzling over when she fell asleep. It was all so simple and so obvious that her failure to grasp the thing sooner made her frown with annoyance. The man was Doran. She should have known it immediately. Of course he was ill. He'd been shot, and by her father's riders, in that fatal pursuit.

She got to her feet. She was surprised, painfully so, to find that she was stiff and cramped. She frowned again and tiptoed across the floor, got down on her hands and knees and fumbled under the bunk until she found the man's boots, which she dragged out. Quickly she examined them for marks of identification and ownership. Cowboys usually initialed or "branded" everything they owned. There was nothing in the first boot that constituted a clue. But inside the second boot she found everything she sought.

There were two initials on the inner rim of the reinforced boot cuff. The boot itself, on the inside as well as the outside, was worn and scuffed, and constant pulling on and yanking off had blurred the telltale letters considerably; however, there was no mistaking or disputing the "DD" burned into the thick, sturdy leather.

There was no joy, no elation within her over her discovery. It was an empty victory—one that left her weak and sick at heart and wishing vainly that she had been mistaken and that the initials had been anvthing but what they were. She did not deny that she had cried loudly for vengeance; that she had demanded that her father's slayer be brought to task for his crime. Denial was useless. But now that he lay within arm's reach of her—helpless, wounded and fever-ridden—there was no vengeance in her heart.

She sank down on the floor. Tears filled her eyes. The boots slid out of her hands. She stared at them with tear-dimmed eyes, turned away from them presently, climbed stiffly and awkwardly to her feet and plodded back to the box. She sat down with a sigh. She leaned forward a bit and rested her elbows on her knees, stared moodily into space and finally cupped her face in her hands. She started when the youthful, grinning face of Bud Watkins suddenly burst into her jumbled thoughts. She sat up with equal suddenness, almost as though someone had come up behind her and jerked her head up. In another minute the "mystery" of Doran began to unravel itself with lightning speed. Bud was the needed key.

Her thoughts went back to an afternoon in her father's tiny office in the ranch house—to Bud's recital of his encounter with Foster and his men, his beating at Foster's hands, his meeting with Doran.

"Dunno exactly what this here Doran feller done tuh Foster an' the others," Bud had said. "All I know is, when I fin'lly come to, Doran was bendin' over me an' the others were gone. I got an idea that they got a look at them Colts he totes—they ain't the kind a tin-horn sports aroun'. Yuh on'y see them on fellers that kin really throw 'em. Mebbe they got a look at his hands an' at the size o' him an' figgered they'd better hightail it while th' hightailin' was good."

The sheriff had his place of importance in the chain of events. Evidently he had started his own individual search for Doran, but whether or not he had found him was something she could not answer. Bud had left her in order to keep an eye on Boone, and from all appearances it was Bud rather than the sheriff who had found Doran. Obviously it was Bud who had repaid his debt to Doran by bringing him to the shack. Then it was Bud, too, who had lighted the lamp and filled the basin with water—it was he who had placed them upon the upended box beside the bunk— it was he who had gotten the wounded man into the makeshift bunk and covered him with the blanket.

It was ironical that, of all places, Doran should find refuge on the Bar-M!

It was even more ironical that she, the daughter of the man whom he had slain, should be the one to minister to him!

She started suddenly when she heard the pounding of galloping horses' hoofs. Quickly she went to the door, opened it and looked out. Her face paled.

A troop of horsemen, strung out in two's, whirled into view. They were headed for the shack. She recognized the two men who rode at the head of the party. One was the sheriff. The other was the burly Foster. She gasped and withdrew her head hastily and slammed the door shut.

CHAPTER TEN
THE SHERIFF LOSES DORAN AGAIN

THE horsemen were some fifty or sixty feet from the shack when the sheriff stiffened suddenly in his saddle and pulled back hard on the reins.

"Pull up!" he yelled.

His horse slid stiff-leggedly to an abrupt, spine-jolting halt. He snorted angrily and pitched viciously for a moment for the reins had been jerked so sharply that the iron bit had cut deep into his lathered jaws. Eight more horses pulled up behind him with equal suddenness. Some of them crowded against those in front of them. There was a bit of a scuffle, with a couple of horses bumping and trampling their mates. Foster quickly backed his mount away when the horse behind him cried out in pain, whirled, reared up and lashed out blindly with his fore hoofs.

His mates shied away from him hastily until his rider calmed him down. Presently the milling subsided. Foster backed his horse into line again and edged him alongside of the sheriff.

"Watcha stoppin' here fer?" he demanded.

The pudgy Boone glanced at him.

"Figgered it'd be smarter if we was tuh leave the posse here," he replied, "while you an' me kinda amble up tuh the shack an' see if Mister Doran's somewheres aroun'."

Foster frowned.

"He's aroun', awright," he said gruffly.

"What makes yuh so all-fire shore?"

"I coulda swore I seen somebody at the door," the big man answered, "an' fer my dough that there somebody wasn't nobody but Doran."

Boone shrugged his shoulder.

"Mebbe," he said presently. "On'y when I seen 'im yest'day he was more dead 'n alive. Still I'm willin' tuh admit he mighta come aroun' by now. Miracles kin happen, an' I ain't the one tuh say they can't."

"Wa-al?"

"Wa-al," the sheriff continued, "if it was him that yuh seen, then there ain't no sense in us bustin' in on 'im sudden-like an' startin' somethin'. My idea is fer the two of us tuh ease ourselves in peaceable-like, see? Then he ain't so li'ble tuh go fer them Colts o' his."

The scowl on Foster's face vanished. "Uh-huh," he said. "I get the idea. Wa-al, Ike—soon's yuh're ready."

Boone swung around in his saddle.

"You fellers," he said, addressing the idling possemen. They looked up shortly. "You fellers stay put. Foster an' me are goin' up tuh the shack fer a look-see. If we need yuh, we'll holler fer yuh. That understood?"

There was a general nodding of heads. The men relaxed in their saddles. The sheriff and Foster dismounted.

"Charley," the latter called.

A man edged his mount forward, caught up their bridles and looped them around his saddle horn. Foster loosened his gun in its holster, whipped it out once and fanned it, nodded fleetingly to himself and shoved it back into the holster. Boone watched him patiently.

"Awright?" he asked.

"Yep."

Together they trudged away. The men followed them with their eyes. Minutes later the two halted in front of the shack. There was a whispered word between Boone and Foster, and then the latter nodded, stepped past the sheriff to the far side of the door, halted and wheeled in one motion. The sheriff glanced at him, raised his right hand and knocked on the door. There was no answer. Boone turned to Foster and shook his head. The burly man caught the sheriff's eye and nodded vigorously. Boone shrugged his shoulder and rapped on the door a second time.

"Yes?"

Boone's eyes widened.

"Who—who is it?" a woman's voice asked.

Foster came at once to Boone's side. The sheriff turned and glared at him.

"So yuh saw Doran at the door, eh?" he demanded scornfully. "I s'ppose that was him that answered?"

Foster frowned.

"Nope," he retorted in a low tone, "but it don't prove that he ain't in there."

"Who is it?" they heard Ann ask again.

Boone motioned to Foster to move away from the door. The big man stepped back reluctantly.

"It's me, Ann—the sheriff."

"The sheriff?" Ann echoed. "Is—is anything wrong?"

"Nope, Honey."

"Oh. Then you won't mind, will you, if I don't open the door? I'm still in bed."

Foster jerked Boone's shirtsleeve.

"How come she's sleepin' here, 'stead of at th' house?" he demanded.

"How'n hell should I know?" Boone snapped irritably. "This shack's hers, same's the house is, so I reckon she kin sleep wherever she wants ter."

"Ask 'er anyway."

The sheriff jerked his arm away.

"Ann," he began presently, "ain't it safer fer yuh tuh bunk up at the house, 'stead of out here by yoreself?"

"Yes, Sheriff, of course it is," she answered promptly. "However, I was caught out here last night in that terrible storm and this was the only shelter I could find."

"Uh-huh," Boone grunted, apparently satisfied with her explanation.

"Ask 'er somethin' 'bout Doran," Foster whispered.

The sheriff turned and gave him a withering stare.

"Go 'head," Foster gritted impatiently.

"I'm leadin' up to it," Boone said through his teeth. "Y'know, Ann—yuh oughtn'ta stray away from the house. Might run inter strangers an' the like—understan'?"

There was no reply from Ann this time. Instead, they heard a step behind the closed door, heard something being shoved away from it, then the door was opened and Ann, a blanket draped around her, appeared in the doorway. As she leaned against the door, both could see everything inside the shack. Their eyes ranged over it. They saw the huge packing case just beyond the door—evidently it had been used to bar the door. A glance at the door revealed that there was no lock on it. Obviously, too, it was the packing case that they had heard being shoved away from the door. They saw the makeshift bunk directly across the floor from the doorway. The bedclothes—what few there were—seemed normally disarranged.

Boone looked up to find Ann's eyes upon him. He flushed awkwardly. She looked past him to Foster, and frowned. Her eyes swept over the big man and shifted back again, almost immediately, to the sheriff. The latter averted his eyes hastily.

"I don't think I have anything to fear from strangers, Sheriff," she said coldly. "It's those I know who might bear watching. Now, if you don't mind—"

Her voice trailed away significantly.

" 'Course, Ann," Boone said quickly, understandingly, and almost apologetically. "Long's yuh're awright, reckon we'd better get goin' again. C'mon, Foster."

The sheriff turned on his heel and trudged away. Foster hitched up his belt, shifted his holster a bit, gave Ann a sidelong glance and marched off. He overtook Boone presently. Ann watched them from the doorway. She saw them tramp up to their horses—saw them mount and wheel—saw the troop clatter away in the direction of McCloud. When they had gone she closed the door.

The bunk was a crude, box-like affair, cot-sized and made of assorted boards which had long since lost whatever similarity they had once had to the usual run of wooden sides of tool crates and packing cases. It had but three sides; the wall against which it had been set up provided the much-needed fourth side.

There were two strips of mattress on the bunk. Once they had formed one full-sized mattress; in order to fit it into the narrow bunk someone had cut it lengthwise, into two equal strips.

In the excitement that followed Ann's sighting of the approaching posse, she recalled having noticed earlier that the mattress consisted of two strips. Quickly she gripped the lower of the two strips, yanked it out from under Doran with a surprising surge of strength and laid it over him full-length. She covered the mattress with the single bed-sheet, a rumpled and badly soiled piece of linen which she handled gingerly. The blanket which had served to cover Doran she had already removed. Quickly she draped it around her, used her newly-found strength to push the packing case against the door, then, strangely calm and unafraid, awaited the posse...

But now that they had passed—now that she knew that she had outwitted them—she felt weak and limp. For a full minute she lay back against the closed door. Then when she felt stronger she unwound the blanket, tore it off and slung it over the packing case and strode to the bunk. She drew away the sheet, pulled back the mattress and looked down. Her eyes widened.

Doran, flat on his back, inches below the level of the bunk's wooden sides and safe from the eyes of anyone standing as Boone and Foster had stood in the doorway, looked up at Ann. He lay there so quietly and motionlessly, his eyes so steady, that he frightened her for a moment. She recoiled unconsciously, frowned when she realized it and bit her lower lip.

"Reckon it's awright fer me tuh get up outa here now?" he asked.

She straightened up slowly.

"Yes," she heard herself reply. "They've gone."

His right hand, big and strong-looking, came up and tightened around the ledge of the bunk. Slowly he pulled himself up into a sitting position. A sudden twinge of pain made him wince. He swung his legs over the side of the bunk and looked down at his stockinged feet.

"Your boots are under the bunk," Ann said.

"Oh," he said simply.

His feet touched the floor. Slowly he attempted to stand. He swayed weakly, unsteadily, for a moment. Ann did not move. He forced himself upright, braced himself on wide-spread legs. His head came up, and their eyes met for a moment. It was Ann who gave ground first; it was she who looked away. She sauntered to the window and looked out. After a minute, when she turned around again, he was sitting on the edge of the bunk, his right boot in his hands. The boot went on with little difficulty; pulling on the left one meant the use of both hands, with the left doing most of the work. He pressed his lips together to stifle the groan that arose in his throat. Swiftly she went to him, took the boot from him, knelt down and helped him draw it on.

"Thank you, Ma'm," he said. "I'm shore obliged to you."

She did not answer. She straightened up, averted her eyes again, turned and picked up her jacket, slipped into it and buttoned it around her.

"I'd advise you to stay here," she said presently, "at least until dark. You'll be safe in leaving then. Follow the river south, to the bend. There's a thicket just beyond it—oh, probably some twenty feet from the bend. You'll find a saddled horse awaiting you there—in the thicket, I mean—and a package of food in the saddle bag. The horse won't be much, so you won't have to worry about returning him."

A quick step brought her to the door. She opened it with a single swift twist of her wrist.

"Just a minute," Doran called.

The door slammed behind her. Doran frowned, made his way to the window and looked out. He spied the girl presently, heard someone hail her and saw her halt abruptly. A mounted man leading a second horse by the bridle hove into view, cantered up to the girl and dismounted in front of her. They talked for a minute, earnestly and quietly; then the man helped her mount the lead horse. She gathered in the reins, settled herself in the saddle, wheeled and rode away. The man looked after her. When she disappeared over a ridge he turned and led his horse toward the shack. When he looked up, Doran recognized him at once. It was Bud Watkins.

CHAPTER ELEVEN
DAN DORAN RIDES AGAIN

T HE youth came striding into the shack presently. He halted in the doorway, spied Doran standing at the window, nodded to him and kicked the door shut.

"Howdy," Doran said.

"How are yuh, Doran? Feelin' more like yoreself?"

"Yeah—reckon so."

Bud pushed his hat up from his eyes and leaned back against the door.

"Tell me somethin'," Doran began. "How'd I get here? You have somethin' tuh do with it?"

"Yep," he replied. "Y'see, I found yuh layin' in some brush, 'bout ready tuh cash in. The sheriff—the ornery polecat—was standin' over yuh with his gun out, all set tuh finish yuh off. I come up behind 'im an'—wa-al, I chased 'im offa the place. I couldn't leave yuh where yuh were, so's he could double back an' do what he was aimin' ter when I homed in, so I boosted yuh up on yore horse an' brought yuh here."

"I see. And who was that girl? Th' one yuh boosted up into the saddle?"

"Don'tcha know?"

Doran shook his head.

"Not yet I don't. She was shore nice-lookin' enough, but she acted doggoned funny."

Bud frowned darkly.

"Reckon if it was the other way 'round—if she'da killed yore ol' man—you'da acted funny tuh her," he replied. Then he added dully, "That was Ann Miller."

There was a puzzled expression on Doran's face.

"Wait a minute, Watkins," he said. "I don't get that—I mean the part about somebody killin' off somebody else's old man."

The youthful cowboy flashed him an odd look. It was evident that he suspected that Doran was bluffing.

"Whatcha tryin' tuh do—kid me?"

"Nope. When it concerns killin', kiddin' is out. Gimme that part all over again," Doran commanded.

Bud hesitated. Obviously he was still unconvinced that he wasn't being kidded.

"Wa-al?" Doran demanded impatiently. "Talk up."

Bud finally shrugged his shoulder.

"Awright," he said heavily. "Ben Miller, Ann's ol' man, was killed in a raid couple o' nights ago. Know anything about it?"

Their eyes met.

"I might," Doran answered calmly. "That is, 'bout the raid. I was in on it—leastways, I was 'mong the raiders. But about the killin'—that's somethin' else again—'less—"

His voice suddenly trailed away. A deep frown spread over his face. For a moment he stared into space.

"Yeah?" Bud demanded quickly. " 'Less what?"

Doran looked up at him again.

"I'm gonna tell yuh the hull thing, Watkins," he said quietly. "Yuh kin b'lieve what I tell yuh or not just as yuh like. But what I'm gonna tell yuh is the truth—understan'?"

"Dunno, but I'm willin' tuh listen. Shoot."

Doran began his story with a recital of the events that followed his arrival in McCloud. He made no mention of his mission to McCloud; he decided that that part could wait for another time. He began with Foster's sudden visit to his hotel, retold the story of their fight in Donlin's, and told Bud of his meeting with

John Sears and of their conversation in the latter's office. He went on to the raid, repeated everything that came to mind. The youth hung onto every word. His eyes never left Doran's face.

"What I'm tryin' tuh tell yuh, Bud," Doran said, "is that I had a doggoned good reason fer joinin' up with Sears. What that reason was, I can't tell yuh right now. The important thing tuh remember is that when my gun went off, I didn't know what was goin' on. Like I said before, I was hit an' hit bad, an' there was on'y one idea in my mind that I kin remember. It was tuh get away. Like I figgered tuh do, I aimed at the horses' legs—not at any o' the riders. Somebody bumped inter me. I remember that an' I remember my gun goin' off. What happened after that— wa-al, I reckon you know all about it a heap better'n I do."

"An' that's th' hull story, eh?"

"Yep. If yuh say I killed Ben Miller, there ain't a thing I kin say tuh deny it. I can't prove I didn't do it."

Bud straightened up. He turned away and paced the floor for a minute. He halted and turned to Doran again presently.

"Doggone it, Doran," he began with a sober shake of his head. "Yuh shore got yoreself inter somethin' awright. Bein' that I wasn't ridin' herd that night, I wasn't 'mong the ones that chased yuh, so I ain't able tuh say whether yuh actu'lly killed ol' Ben or yuh didn't. All I know is what the others tol' me. But s'pposin' I'm willin' tuh believe yuh—then, outside o' me, who'n hell else d'yuh s'ppose'll be willin' tuh admit that mebbe yuh didn't mean tuh kill Ben—huh?"

"Nobody."

The youth nodded.

"There yuh are. Oh, yeah, Doran—there's somethin' puzzlin' me. Mebbe you kin kinda supply the answers I'm lookin' fer—huh?"

"I kin try. What's on yore mind?"

"Wa-al, first off, it concerns that polecat Boone—the sheriff. Yest'day he was fixin' tuh kill yuh. Today he an' his posse are out lookin' fer yuh. Now what I don't savvy is this. Both of yuh take yore orders from the same feller —that skunk Sears. Right? That bein' so—how come? What's behind all this? Sears give yuh a job one day an' send Boone out tuh kill yuh the next?"

Doran shook his head.

"Dunno yet, Bud. Leastways th' answers yuh want don't come tuh me right off."

"H'm," the youth muttered. Then, in a louder voice, "Understan' Ann tol' yuh tuh stay put here till dark an' tuh high-tail it away then. That right?"

Doran nodded.

"On'y I don't aim tuh go anywheres."

"Huh? Yuh don't?" Bud's eyes widened. "Then what do yuh aim tuh do?"

"That gun yuh got stickin' outa yore pants belt—that one of mine?" Doran asked.

"The gun?" the youth repeated. "Oh, yeah, shore. Foun' it layin' in the grass. Meant tuh put it inter the empty holster on yore belt. Reckon I musta fergot about it in all the excitement."

"Then you know where my belt is?"

" 'Course I do. Took it off yuh before I got yuh inter bed. It's under the bunk, up against the wall. I'll get it fer yuh."

"Willya?"

Bud strode to the bunk, got down on his knees and fumbled underneath the home-made bed for a minute. He grunted presently and backed away from it, Doran's gun-belt in his hand, and climbed to his feet.

"Here yuh are."

"Oh, much obliged."

Doran buckled the belt around his waist. There was a gun in one holster. Bud jerked its mate out of his pants belt and banded it over mutely. He watched gravely as Doran hefted and shoved it into the empty holster. Doran looked up. There was a trace of a smile on his face.

"That's better," he said lightly. "When a feller gets used ter the feel of a holster swingin' against his thighs, bein' without 'em makes 'im feel like he's on'y part dressed."

The youth nodded understandingly.

"Got any idea what become o' Bess?" Doran asked.

"Who? Bess? Oh—yuh mean yore horse?"

"Uh-huh."

"Oh," Bud said quickly. "She's awright. Yuh got a real horse there, Doran. Say—did yuh know she had a bad nick in 'er leg?"

"Bullet crease?"

"Yeah. I fixed it up. Reckon it won't bother 'er much," Bud replied.

"Yuh're awright, Watkins. I shore owe yuh a-plenty. Where's Bess at?"

"Got 'er hid away. Figgered it'd be safer fer 'er, case somebody like Boone foun' 'er an' kinda took a shine tuh 'er. You kin go get 'er tuhnight."

It was a clear, moonlit night. A cool breeze raced over the river from the distant hills and turned inland. Doran tramped along the river bank, turning frequently to look back. He had hoped that Bud Watkins, leading Bess by her bridle, would over-take him and save him the trouble of making the two-mile trek to the river bend where they had agreed to meet. The ground was soft and muddy as a result of the storm of the previous night, and the grass was soggy, all of which made walking in high-heeled boots a hardship. He halted more frequently now and looked back, listening intently, but there was no echoing clatter or grass-muffled pounding of horses' hoofs. He frowned and wondered if the youth had been delayed; or if he had run into trouble.

Then he suddenly recalled what the youth had told him. He had hidden Bess away in a distant ravine. That would mean that Bud, after "picking up" the mare, would have to come across country in an effort to save time. In that event he would doubt-less strike directly for the bend rather than aim for a spot north of it and thus follow the river bank as he had instructed Doran to do. Doran realized that it was he, rather than Bud, who would be late. He quickened his pace instantly.

He scowled darkly, angrily, as he plodded along. The faces of Sears and Foster flashed through his jumbled thoughts. He cursed them both, cursed them individually and collectively. He doubled his big fists, and gave vent to his anger by pounding his right fist into his left palm with a viciousness that boded ill for both Sears and Foster. He looked up suddenly, forgetting the two men for that moment. Ahead of him the river seemed to swing sharply inland, disappearing from sight around a bend.

"Reckon that's it, awright," he muttered. He whistled shrilly. There was no reply. "Guess he ain't come yet. Still, I don't s'ppose it'll be more'n a couple o' minutes before he shows up."

He heard a rush of hoofs somewhere behind him and turned quickly. His eyes probed the darkness. The pounding grew louder. Presently a shadowy horseman leading a riderless horse rode out of the night. The youth hadn't failed him. The lead horse—it was Bess of course—whinnied. It was music to Doran's ears. His spir-its soared.

"Bud!" he yelled.

He dashed forward. His legs had seemed leaden but a minute before; now they were springy and strong. He raced over the soft, muddy earth that had clung to his boots and the wet, limp grass that had yielded beneath his every step, disregarding them com-pletely as he darted toward the approaching horses. They slid to a halt presently, and Doran came panting up to them.

"That's what I call timin' it, awright," he gasped breathlessly. "Right down tuh the minute, too. I shore am obliged tuh yuh, Bud. Hope I get a chance, an' pronto, too, tuh do somethin' fer you in return."

"You've got that chance right now," he heard a voice say in reply. But it wasn't Bud Watkins' voice. It was a girl's voice—Ann Miller's.

"Oh," he said lamely. "Thought yuh were Bud—Bud Watkins."

"I'm sorry to disappoint you," she said coldly, "but Bud couldn't come. He's disappeared."

He eyed her sharply.

"What d'yuh mean—he's disappeared?" he demanded.

"Just that," she replied evenly. "I think your employer, the very honorable John Sears, can tell you more. You might ask him."

He scowled darkly.

"You tryin' tuh tell me that Bud's been kidnapped?" he asked.

"You can draw your own conclusions."

"H'm."

He reached for the reins, took them from her without a word, whirled around her horse and climbed into his own saddle. He wheeled the mare.

"I suppose I ought to tell you what I think of you," he heard her say, "but what good would it do? I'm sure it's nothing new for you, having someone tell you that they loathe you, despise you—that you're low and contemptible."

"Anythin' else?"

"No!"

"Awright then. You've had yore say an' I reckon I know what yuh think o' me. S'ppose we leave things the way they are—fer the time bein' anyway. Mebbe some other time we kin kinda go over 'em again. Right now I got things tuh 'tend to in McCloud, so I'm headin' fer there pronto. As fer you, ma'am, I'm gonna suggest, whether yuh want me tuh or not, that yuh make tracks fer home an' that yuh stay put there so's nuthin' kin happen to yuh."

The mare bounded away. Her flashing hoofs echoed over the range for a brief minute; then the night swallowed her and the range was hushed again.

CHAPTER TWELVE
WHEN A MAN'S A MAN

JAKE EARLY, Ike Boone's deputy, dozed fitfully in the chair behind the sheriff's desk. Jake's bald head was bowed, and his bristly, unshaven chin thumped against his flat chest each time he drew a breath.

Under normal conditions, that is, when there were no prisoners in the cellblock, Jake generally retired to his own quarters at sundown and went to sleep. Undisturbed, Jake could sleep around the clock with little or no effort. But now there was a prisoner in the block to be guarded and looked in on every now and then. The thought of it prevented Jake from going to bed. Instead, he was forced to doze in the chair behind the sheriff's desk. He grumbled about it every time he opened his eyes and listened. Then, too, he recalled the sheriff's threat to "kick his teeth out" if the prisoner managed to break out of the place. Jake's teeth were few and he had an overpowering desire to retain them; hence he made frequent though begrudging trips back to Bud Watkins' cell.

Jake opened one eye when he heard a knock on the door. He frowned and lowered his legs to the floor and sat up.

"C'min!" he called gruffly.

The door did not open. Then he remembered that he had bolted it. He mumbled something under his breath, pushed his chair back from the desk and got up. His right leg had developed a cramp, and he winced and rubbed it briskly for a minute, stamped it and finally plodded to the door. He pulled back the slide bolt and jerked the door open.

"Wa-al?" he demanded.

He blinked. There was no one at the door. He frowned and slammed it shut, mumbled again and trudged back to the chair. He swung it around and sank into it and closed his eyes. He stretched his legs and sighed. He had left the door unlocked. If the person who had knocked returned, Jake wouldn't have to admit him. He could admit himself. Jake opened his eyes when he heard the knock on the door again.

"C'min—drat yuh!" he yelled.

He turned slowly and glared at the door. It did not open.

"Think they're funny," he mumbled to himself.

He was certain that it was some of the cowboys playing one of their tricks.

"Them fellers never'll grow up," he muttered. He waited another minute. "Wa-al, c'min!"

He scowled darkly. He was annoyed now. He climbed to his feet and strode to the door and jerked it open. For a moment he was quiet, motionless, poised in the doorway; then he marched out, and darted around the building to a dark alley beside it.

"You blamed fools!" he yelled.

The alley was dark and he could see nothing in it, but he was definitely convinced that the playful punchers had taken refuge there, safe from his angry, probing eyes; he was equally certain that the shadows in the alley were man-made.

"Come outa there, yuh polecats!" he yelled. "I kin see yuh!"

There was no reply to his invitation, no shuffling of booted feet. He frowned darkly. They were in there, he told himself, huddling in the darkness against the fence, or against the side of the building itself, chuckling and laughing among themselves. He cursed them, cursed his helplessness and turned away slowly, but he halted again almost immediately when he spied a can lying just within the entrance to the alley. The tin can gleamed brightly in the night light. As he stared at it, an idea came to him.

Swiftly he bent and picked up the can. It was empty. A bit of a smile swept over his face.

"Awright," he muttered. "Yuh asked fer it, y'know. Now let's hear yuh laugh it off."

He drew back his arm and hurled the can into the alley. He was surprised—more than that, he was disappointed —when there was no immediate howl of pain from within the alley. He heard the can strike the ground, heard it bound against the fence. He scowled again, turned and trudged into the office and slammed the door behind him.

A gun was suddenly jammed hard against his ribs.

"Awright," he heard a voice say coldly. "Stand where yuh are."

Jake jerked to a halt. He gulped and swallowed hard. There was no playfulness in the voice of the man behind the gun; certainly there was none in the way he had slammed the gun against the deputy's ribs. A muscular arm came around him. Jake stared at it with widened eyes. A hand ran over him, probing for a gun, made its way up and under his armpits in search of a hidden shoulder holster; finding none, the hand was withdrawn. Jake heard the bolt on the door slide home.

"Yuh all alone?"

The deputy tried to answer. There was a curious rumble in his suddenly parched throat, but that was all. He managed to nod.

"Where's Watkins?"

Jake gulped again.

"Down—down there."

He nodded toward the cell block beyond the office.

"Lead the way," the cold voice commanded. "If yuh don't aim tuh join yore ancestors 'head o' time, don't try any tricks. Savvy?"

"Sh-shore."

"Go 'head then."

Jake plodded forward. The man with the gun kept close behind him. Jake could almost feel his breath on his neck. He halted presently in front of a barred cell door. It was the last one in the block.

"He's in there," he said.

He jerked his head toward the cell on his right, indicating that that was the cell in which Watkins was confined. He was suddenly possessed of a fear that he would be struck over the head with the barrel or butt of his captor's gun, and he winced inwardly in anticipation of the blow. He was suddenly and roughly pushed away. He stumbled awkwardly and collided heavily with the barred door of the cell opposite Watkins', grabbed the bars and saved himself from falling. He twisted around and got a glimpse of the man who had pushed him. He was a stranger. He was tall and blond and broad-shouldered.

"Bud!" he heard the man call.

Jake managed to look into Watkins' cell. The prisoner was sprawled out on his cot. The tall man banged on the door's bars with the barrel of his gun.

"Bud! Get up!"

The youth turned over, grunted and opened his eyes.

"Huh?"

He blinked and rubbed his eyes.

"Oh—Doran!"

"C'mon, kid—yuh wanna get outa here, don'tcha?"

"An' how." The youth laughed lightly. He was wide awake now. He swung his legs over the side of the cot. He looked up at Doran. "Y'know, I had a feelin' that yuh'd come fer me soon's yuh foun' out what happened tuh me."

Doran turned to Jake.

"Open 'er up," he ordered.

Jake fumbled in his pocket for a moment. He finally produced a huge key. Doran snatched it out of his hand, holstered his gun, inserted the key in the lock of the cell door, turned it and pulled the door open. It creaked loudly.

"Awright, Bud," Doran said. "Hop outta there, will yuh? Got a feller out here lookin' fer 'ccommodations fer the night, an' there ain't any sense keepin' 'im waitin'."

Watkins grinned and got to his feet. He stretched himself, hitched up his pants, picked up his hat and sauntered out. Doran looked at Jake again.

"Go 'head, mister," he said curtly. "Help yoreself."

Jake managed a sickly grin and shuffled forward. He brushed past Watkins, past Doran, and stepped into the cell. The door was slammed behind him. He heard the key grate in the lock.

"Let's go," he heard Doran say.

He heard them stride away, heard the street door open and close. Jake felt easier now. He looked down at the cot and grinned lightly.

"This is turnin' out a heap better'n I figgered it would," he muttered. " 'Course th' sheriff'll raise hell, but he'll get over it. An' if he don't—wa-al—"

His voice trailed away. He was tired, and it was an effort for him to keep his eyes open. He yawned and stretched himself, scratched his left ear and rubbed his nose and sat down on the edge of the cot. He yawned again, kicked off his boots, opened his belt and sank down. He shifted himself a bit until his head was completely comfortable; then he sighed deeply, wearily, and closed his eyes.

In the shadowy darkness of an alley far down the street, Doran and Bud Watkins conversed in low tones. A few feet behind them concealed by the protective darkness too, were two horses—Bess and another. Doran had already explained that he had "found" the second horse idling along the street.

"Dunno who owns the critter," Doran was saying, "but who-ever he belongs tuh ain't one tuh throw 'way money buyin' feed fer 'im. That there horse ain't nuthin' but skin an' bones, an' if you throw just one square meal into 'im, you'll 've paid fer usin' 'im. Hop on 'im, Bud, an' get outa here. That Miller girl's probably worried half tuh death over yuh by now, so get goin'. Ain't no sense in keepin' her in a stew any longer'n necessary, y'know. Like's not she's a'ready figgered that the worst's happened to yuh."

Bud grunted, hitched up his belt and turned toward the waiting horse. He caught up the reins, hesitated, turned to Doran again and flashed him a questioning look.

"Wa-al? What's the matter now?"

"Nuthin'," the youth replied. "On'y what about you? How come you ain't pullin' outa here now too?"

"Me? Oh, got some bus'ness here that kinda needs 'ttendin' tuh, an' I reckon this is about as good a time fer it as any," Doran said lightly.

"H'm. That there bus'ness o' yourn got anything tuh do with a couple o' polecats named Sears an' Foster?"

Doran laughed softly.

"In a way."

Bud grunted.

"That's what I figgered. Hope yuh ain't aimin' tuh take 'em both on at the same time. Yuh ain't fergot about that bum shoulder o' yourn, have yuh?"

"Not much chance o' me fergettin' that so soon, Bud. Besides, what gives yuh the idea that I'm plannin' tuh do anything, huh?"

"Oh—just an idea I got."

"Ferget it, then. You just hop 'board that there critter an' head fer th' Bar-M."

"Awright," the youth said heavily. "Reckon yuh're the boss. So long, Doran."

"So long, kid. Watch yore step."

"Better watch yore own," Bud said over his shoulder.

He rode out of the darkened alleyway, turned in his saddle and looked back, swung into the street and jogged away.

CHAPTER THIRTEEN
DORAN STATES HIS CASE

DORAN was grateful for the lateness of the hour and the darkness of the night. He pulled the brim of his hat far down over his eyes, looked around casually and sauntered off. Fortunately, most of the town's stores had already closed, and he kept close to the buildings in order to take advantage of their protective darkness. The saloons of course were still open, and he quickened his pace and turned his head each time he came abreast of one. Loud voices and equally loud laughter, and here and there a brief snatch of a gay, lilting tune, floated streetward through the open doors.

He strode briskly past Donlin's and nearly collided with a man who came staggering out of the place. Doran swerved sharply toward the curb in order to avoid him. The man turned and looked after him, swayed on unsteady legs and finally called to him, but Doran paid no attention. The drunk cursed and turned slowly, an awkward maneuver in the course of which he nearly fell down, and plodded away uncertainly in the opposite direction. Doran looked back at him over his shoulder, a quick glance prompted by curiosity, and saw him stagger into another saloon some twenty or thirty feet down the street from Donlin's. Then, his curiosity apparently satisfied, Doran went on his way again.

Minutes later he came abreast of the sheriff's office. He gave it a sidelong glance and grinned lightly. There was no immediate sign of life or activity about the place; everything seemed quiet and normal, at least outwardly. He plodded past it, went past the darkened alley which ran parallel to the structure and looked up again. Just ahead of him was the building which housed John Sears' office. The grin vanished instantly. His lips thinned and his eyes glinted when he noticed a light in the county attorney's office. He slackened his pace when he spied a man idling in front of the building.

"Uh-huh," he muttered to himself. "Got a feller standin' guard in front o' the door so's nobody kin barge in on 'em sudden-like. Must be havin' an important powwow upstairs. Wonder what kind o' hell they're cookin' up now?"

Doran's pace became a casual saunter. The guard, his thumbs hooked in his gun belt, looked up when he heard Doran's step. The latter halted in front of him.

"Got a match on yuh, partner?" Doran asked.

The man eyed him.

"Yeah," he said finally. "Reckon so."

He thrust his hands into his pockets, fumbled in them for a moment. The blunt muzzle of a big Colt suddenly dug deep into his ample stomach. He jerked his hands out of his pockets instinctively.

"Hey, what the—" he began.

"Shut up," Doran snapped. " 'Less yuh're plumb tired o' livin', keep yore mouth shut tight an' do's yuh're told. Get it? Awright, then. Now back up tuh that door behind yuh. Go 'head."

The man hesitated for a moment, until Doran prodded him with his gun; then he started to back up. In an instant they were directly in front of the door, with the captive's shoulders actually touching the wooden panels.

"Awright," Doran said gruffly. "I'll open it."

He reached around the man and tried the door. It was unlocked; it opened easily and, fortunately, noiselessly. Just inside was a darkened vestibule, beyond it a short flight of stairs leading to the upper floor. A dim light burned on the landing above.

"Turn aroun'," Doran commanded.

The man grunted and turned slowly. Doran swiftly jerked the gun out of the guard's holster and shoved it into his own belt.

"Go 'head," he said shortly. "Inside."

The man obeyed, this time without any hesitancy whatso-ever. The loss of his own gun, together with the persistent prod-ding of Doran's, left him no alternative. Doran, right at his heels, crowded in behind him and quietly closed the door.

"Now listen tuh me, partner," Doran began in a low tone. "We're goin' upstairs—see? I'll tell yuh when tuh start an' what tuh do, so's there won't be 'ny chance f'r yuh t' make a mistake. Y'see, this finger o' mine is kinda nervous an' itchy tuh night, an' there's no tellin' just when it's li'ble tuh pull the trigger an' scatter yore carcass all over the place."

There was no comment from the man.

"First off, who's upstairs?" Doran asked.

"Nobody."

"Yuh're a liar."

"Awright—Sears is up in 'is office."

"Uh-huh—an' who's he powwowin' with?"

"The sheriff."

"Ain't yuh fergettin' Foster?"

"Oh, yeah. Come tuh think of it, he's up there, too."

"That's what I figgered," Doran said dryly. "Awright, reckon we kin get goin' now. When I jab yuh with my gun stop right where yuh are. Get it?"

The man grunted.

"G'wan then."

The man hitched up his belt. Slowly, almost methodically, he led the way into the dimly lighted hallway; then he mounted the stairs. He hesitated momentarily on the second step.

"Go 'head," Doran ordered.

The man went on again. Doran followed at his heels. The wooden stairs, evidently badly warped, creaked beneath them. Doran matched steps with his captive in an effort to create the impression that but one man was ascending. Slowly they climbed the stairs; then they were on the landing. Sears' office—the only one on the upper floor—was on the left. The man halted when Doran jabbed him sharply with his gun.

"Knock on the door," Doran whispered. "Whoever answers or opens the door—tell 'im yuh wanna see Foster. Understan'?"

The man nodded. Doran nudged him, and he tramped up to the door. Doran, catlike, whirled past him and flattened out against the blank wall just beyond the closed office door. The man raised his hand and knocked.

"Yeah?" a gruff voice demanded from within the office.

"It's me, Sheriff," Doran's prisoner replied. "Carson."

"Wa-al?"

"Kin I see Foster fer a minute?"

There was a moment's wait for the sheriff's reply.

"Awright. C'min."

Carson glanced quickly, questioningly at Doran. The latter nodded mutely. Carson opened the door. Doran stepped directly behind him. He got a fleeting glimpse of the office and of the three men sitting around the county attorney's desk—Sears behind it and Foster and Boone on the opposite side of it, facing him. Now the three men looked up. Doran gave Carson a sudden, powerful shove and sent him stumbling into the office. The guard fell against the desk. Foster and Boone bounded to their feet.

"What the—" Foster began.

His right hand darted toward his holster.

"Hold it!" Doran snapped.

He was over the threshold and inside the office; now both of his Colts gleamed in his hands. Foster's hand halted in midair, inches from his gun butt.

"Sit down," Doran commanded.

Foster and Boone slowly seated themselves again.

"Both of yuh keep yore hands up on the desk," Doran said presently. "You—Sears—don't try tuh reach that shoulder holster inside yore coat 'less yuh're plannin' tuh commit suicide."

Sears frowned darkly. He gave Doran an icy stare, sank back in his chair and folded his arms across his chest. Doran backed up slowly and kicked the door shut.

"Awright, Carson," he said. "Find yoreself a place some-where's off tuh a side an' stay put there. Yuh'll live longer if yuh keep outa things."

Carson grunted. He straightened up and rubbed his right arm, gently at first, vigorously when he saw that the others were looking at him. There was a chair standing against the far wall of the office. Carson looked at it, glanced at Doran, trudged across the room and swung the chair away from the wall. Cowboy-like he tilted it against the wall, seated himself, hooked his boot heels in the rungs of the chair and looked up.

"Awright, you fellers," Doran began. "Mebbe now we kin kinda get down tuh cases. Sheriff—"

Boone gulped and jerked his head up. From the expression on his face it was evident that he expected the very worst. His eyes seemed to focus on the blunt muzzles of Doran's guns, as though he expected a leaden blast from them.

"I heard 'bout yuh 'rrestin' the Watkins kid," Doran went on. Boone raised his eyes. " 'Course I knew it was on'y a frame-up an' that it wasn't on account o' him doin' anythin', 'less stoppin' an ornery skunk from committin' murder like you was fixin' tuh do is against the law. Anyway, Boone, I stopped off at yore place first thing. I found the kid cooped up there. He looked so doggoned uncomfortable sprawled out on a busted-down cot that I let 'im out an' sent 'im home."

The sheriff swallowed hard. He half arose.

"Sit down," Doran said curtly.

Boone flushed, averted his eyes and sat down again.

"Awright, Sears," Doran said. "Got a couple o' things tuh say tuh you now."

A sigh of relief escaped Boone. Doran was finished with him.

"Sears," Doran began presently, "I've been lookin' at yuh an' studyin' yuh an' wonderin' what yuh remind me of. I know what it is now—a wolf."

Sears' lean, clean-shaven face grew hard and cold. Beneath his chalky cheeks, tensed jaw muscles twitched with rage.

"When Watkins tol' me how Boone tried tuh kill me," Doran continued, "I was kinda stumped. I couldn't figger it out, since both of us were s'pposed tuh be workin' fer the same boss. But shucks, Sears—I musta been dumber'n hell not tuh expect some kind o' crookedness with you holdin' a hand in this game. Fact is, I'm plumb disgusted with myself fer havin' tuh puzzle over somethin' that a baby coulda doped out between feedin's."

"Really?"

"Yeah. Sears, yuh're overrated. You ain't half as smart's yuh're s'pposed tuh be—heck, no. Yuh can't be, because what yuh had in mind is just as plain tuh me as the nose on Boone's face."

Boone frowned and looked away. Carson caught his eyes and grinned. The sheriff gave him an icy stare, and Carson colored, lowered his eyes and coughed lightly behind his hand.

"Sears," Doran droned, "yuh figgered I'd do some talkin' if the Bar-M bunch got hold o' me. Yuh were worried that I might tell 'em that you—the county attorney—had hired me tuh do some killin' fer yuh. Yuh couldn't rest till yuh knew fer shore that I was dead, so yuh sent Boone out tuh find me, an' yuh musta tol' 'im that if I wasn't dead a'ready, he was tuh put the finishin' touches tuh me."

Sears smiled coldly.

"That's very interesting, Doran," he said lightly. "Pray continue. Your deductions fascinate me."

"That so?" Doran drawled. "Wa-al, go 'head, then, an' keep on enjoyin' yoreself while yuh kin. Life's li'ble tuh be awful short, y'know. Anyway, lucky fer me an' unlucky's hell fer you, young Watkins come along an' chased Boone offa the Bar-M."

The sheriff snorted loudly.

"H'm," he sputtered. "The hell he did."

Doran glanced at him, and he subsided.

"Now," Doran continued, "tuh show Boone an' Foster what kin happen tuh them when yuh figger they've kinda outlived their usefulness to yuh—when yuh heard 'bout me killin' off Ben Miller, which musta been even more than yuh'd hoped anyone'd do, yuh decided it'd be a good idea tuh get rid o' me, too. It wasn't on'y on account o' what I might spill if I got caught; heck, yuh were lookin' ahead. You were afraid that if I got away with a hull skin I might get too big fer my britches an' that I might kinda get the idea that I was entitled tuh some o' the gravy you an' Boone've been wallowin' in fer so long."

Sears laughed lightly.

"Have you finished, Mister Doran?" he asked.

"Nope," Doran replied. "You'll know when I'm done —yuh won't hafta ask. Sheriff, if yuh ever expect tuh get me, reckon this is the time fer yuh tuh act. Let's see the stuff yuh're s'pposed tuh be made of—step right up an' help yoreself."

Boone scowled darkly; however, he made no attempt to accept Doran's invitation.

"Mebbe yore side-partner, Foster,'d be glad tuh lend a hand. What d'yuh say, Foster?"

There was no response from the burly man—nothing but a murderous glare. Doran laughed.

"Sears, yuh ain't even good at hirin' help," he said tauntingly. "Lookit them two mavericks. They're scared tuh death. The three of yuh shore make a fine gang, awright—two coyotes an' a wolf an' none of yuh got the guts of a louse."

Doran holstered his guns. The four men—one of them wide-eyed and spellbound, the others grim-faced and sullen—watched him. He hooked his thumbs in his belt casually.

"Oh, yeah," he said as an afterthought. "I aim tuh stay 'round M'Cloud fer quite a spell. How long depends —wa-al, on a heap o' things. Anyway, you polecats keep outa my way. I'm li'ble tuh bite's well as bark the next time I see yuh—savvy?"

He turned toward the door, halted again and looked back.

"An' here's a tip in case any of yuh get the idea that yuh might like tuh take somethin' out on Bud Watkins—just fer spite, y'know. Wa-al, the feller that fergets this warnin' is shore gonna wish he'da remembered. Leave the kid alone—understan'?"

No one answered, and no one moved for a moment. The room was hushed, oppressively and heavily silent; then Doran broke the spell.

He opened the door, swung it wide and started out, only to jerk himself backward and whirl sideways. The light on the landing had been turned out, plunging the hallway into total darkness.

A gun roared, and a bullet ploughed into the door. It tore through a wooden panel, leaving a jagged hole less than an inch to the left of Doran's shoulder. Doran fired from the hips. Flame stabbed the darkened landing. Gun thunder rocked the room and smoke thickened the air.

Foster leaped to his feet.

"Give it to 'im!" he yelled.

He jerked out his gun and snapped a shot at Doran, but the latter ducked, almost instinctively, and ripped a single shot at the burly man in angry reply. Foster's hat was torn off his head. He tried desperately to whirl out of range, certain that a second shot would follow, fell over his own chair and went down heavily.

Doran's guns thundered again, a blast of deadly lead that swept the landing. Blue smoke swirled up and around him. Now a shadowy figure stumbled out of the darkness and groped his way to the open doorway. The newcomer's face was a bloody mass. The man halted on the threshold, swayed on buckling legs and suddenly pitched forward into the office. Doran, on the alert, sidestepped. The man struck the floor and rolled over. Doran hurdled him and leaped out.

Now it was Ike Boone's turn. Gun in hand, he ran toward the door, stepped over the motionless man on the floor and fired twice at a shadow on the landing. Boone cursed when he heard Doran's step on the stairs. He heard the street door open—heard it slam behind Doran.

Doran halted for a moment in front of the building. He was curious to see if the shooting had attracted anyone's attention. His fears were quickly dissipated. The street was hushed, deserted and dark, save for two dimly lighted saloons in the middle of the block. He heard laughter and one or two voices, but the noise of the earlier part of the evening was lacking. It was late, even for McCloud. Then, too, it was evident that liquor had had its effect on the patrons.

He looked up at Sears' window. The light had been turned out. He edged away from the door, watching the window above him carefully, then suddenly bolted and dashed up the street, keeping close to the darkened buildings as he raced away.

Somewhere behind him, perhaps a bit above him, too, a gun suddenly roared and a hail of lead sprayed the sidewalk about him. A bullet whined past him, and an instant later a store window beyond him fell in with a deafening crash. He looked back over his shoulder and snapped a shot at what appeared to be the head and shoulders of a man who was leaning out of the county attorney's window.

Half a dozen men poured out of a saloon, halted and looked up and down the street. Two or three women with shawls thrown around their barcd shoulders pushed past them to the curb. A gun again spat fire from Sears' window. Then one of the women spied Doran running up the street.

"Over there!" she cried, pointing to him excitedly. "That man—see him?"

A man behind her shouldered her out of the way and strode into the gutter. He waited until Doran came abreast of him.

"Hey, you!" he called. "Hol' on there a minute! Wanna talk tuh yuh!"

Doran never slackened his pace. Now a burly figure burst out of the building far down the end of the street. It was Foster, gun in hand. He caught a glimpse of Doran racing along the sidewalk. He fired twice, three times, each shot hard upon the echo of the one before it, but his fire was erratic and wild. He spied the man in the middle of the gutter.

"Get that feller!" he yelled.

The man whipped out his gun and fired. Doran, some twenty feet up the street from him, wheeled suddenly and flamed a leaden answer. The man dropped his gun and clutched at his right wrist. His companions, headed by the women, came dashing to his side and crowded around him.

Foster lumbered up a moment later.

"Where'd—where'd that feller go?" he demanded breathlessly.

One of the men looked up.

"Huh? Oh. Dunno, Foster. Reckon we kinda fergot tuh notice," he replied.

"Why, yuh dumb fool!" Foster exploded.

He swung away abruptly and loped off again. Minutes later he panted up to the very end of the street and looked about him. A frown spread over his face.

There was no sign of Doran. He had disappeared.

CHAPTER FOURTEEN
MARY DONLIN

DORAN saw the man drop his gun. He was finished; there would be no further interference on his part. Doran shot a backward glance over his shoulder. For a moment he watched a bulky figure galloping up the street. There was no mistaking the lumbering runner.

"Uh-huh—Foster, awright," Doran muttered, eyeing him. "Runs from side tuh side like a lopsided stage."

He wheeled finally and raced off. He was still half a block away from the alley in which he had left Bess. He realized that it would be foolhardy for him to head directly for the alley; Foster would be certain to follow him, if not all the way, then far enough to thwart immediate escape. The burly man would raise a hullabaloo, the townsmen would snatch up their guns and come tumbling into the street, and Doran would be trapped.

He would have to take a more circuitous route to avoid being followed; then, once he had gained the temporary safety of the darkened alley, he would have to bide his time until he felt that it was either safe enough to venture out or imperative that he make a break for it, regardless of circumstances. In either case, escape would then depend upon the fleet-footed Bess.

This section of the street was dark and gloomy and shadowy, with dirty-windowed stores and drab shacks silent and lifeless in the night light. Their proprietors and tenants, as the case might be, had long since turned in, and now not a single light was visible in any of them. Doran kept close to them, grateful for the protective screen of darkness they provided. He swerved sharply toward the curb when a door in a shack just ahead of him opened suddenly. Instantly his gun swept upward, poised and ready to blast away at anyone who might seek to stop him.

"Around the side!" he heard a woman's voice say. "Hurry!"

He skidded to a hesitant, doubtful halt. This had all the earmarks of a trap, yet—

Framed in the doorway was the figure of a woman silhouetted against a background of dim, shaded light from within the shack.

"Come in," she said quickly.

"Awright."

She held the door wide. In another moment he was over the threshold and into the shack. He wheeled when he heard the door close and saw her bolt it. She turned presently, her back against the door, and looked up at him. Their eyes met. There hadn't been time for him to look at her before; now that there was, he proceeded to take advantage of the opportunity.

She was pretty—no doubt about that. He judged her age as about thirty-five.

"Thanks fer askin' me in, Ma'am," he began. "Hope yuh don't get inter trouble over it."

She smiled wanly.

"It's quite all right, I assure you," she replied. Her eyes ranged over him. "You're Doran, aren't you?"

He nodded.

"Uh-huh. How'd yuh know?"

"I didn't, really," she said brightly. "I just hoped you were."

"Oh," he said, and pretended to be satisfied with her answer.

Now he was firmly convinced that he had rushed into a trap. It was the kind of set-up that only a calculating mind such as John Sears' could have arranged. It was evident that the county attorney had expected him to return—he had even prepared for the possibility that Doran might shoot his way to freedom despite Foster and Boone and the guard—and in order to detain him in such an eventuality, he had installed the woman in the shack, perhaps furnished her with a description of Doran and instructed her to be on the alert for gunfire.

When it broke out she would know that Doran had appeared; she would know too that he had gotten away and that it was up to her to lure him into the shack and detain him there until—

"Your horse," the woman said, and interrupted his deductions. He looked up quickly. "He's in the shed behind the house."

"That so?"

He was surprised, but he managed somehow to veil his feelings. He smiled lightly, waiting patiently for her to continue.

"He'll be safe there," she went on, "in case they search the town."

He eyed her curiously.

"What's tuh stop 'em from lookin' 'round here, too?" he asked.

She shook her head.

"They won't come here," she said calmly.

"No?"

"No," she said with finality.

He shrugged his broad shoulders.

"Awright—if you say so."

"Did you—did you kill John Sears?" she asked.

"Sears?" he repeated. He shook his head. "Nope."

She was silent now; he watched her, wondering what she was thinking. She raised her eyes again presently.

"Doran," she began, "if I help you get away safely, will you do something for me in return?"

He looked at her sharply. He was puzzled now. Was it possible that he had misjudged things?

"Well?" she asked presently.

"Huh? Oh, yeah—shore, Ma'am. What d'yuh want me tuh do?"

"The Bar-M is to be raided," she said quietly. "It's to be wiped out this time."

He started, but checked himself almost instantly.

"Yuh don't say?"

He was still trying to appear unaffected. He forced himself to wait for her to continue, but impatience overcame him finally. "Wa-al, what's the Bar-M an' the fact that it's gonna be raided got tuh do with me?"

"Nothing," she said calmly. "Unless you want it to have something to do with you."

"What d'yuh mean?"

"Well," she began again, this time just a bit hesitantly, "if they were forewarned—"

"Uh-huh—they could do somethin' about it, right?"

"They might be able to save themselves," she concluded.

"H'm." He looked at her through narrowed lids. "How d'yuh know this here raid's really comin' off?"

"I just know it is. You'll have to take my word for it."

"An' when's it s'pposed tuh be?"

"At dawn."

"Tomorrer?"

"It's tomorrow now," she replied. "It has been for more than three hours."

"Oh, yeah? Reckon there ain't much time tuh lose, if I'm gonna go warn 'em, is there?"

"No—none."

He frowned in thought. She waited patiently, quietly, apparently content to allow him to decide things for himself.

"Awright," he grunted finally. "I'll go."

She turned without a word and fumbled with the bolt on the door. He pretended not to notice; it gave him an opportunity to look around the place. He noted that it was but a one-room

TROUBLE AT MOON PASS

affair and a poorly furnished one at that. He ran his eyes over the furnishings quickly—noted an old, worn bureau against one wall and a hard, straight-backed chair just beyond it. Against the opposite wall stood an iron bedstead. In a corner of the room was a small table, and on top of it a heavily shaded lamp, the sole source of light for the shack. There was but one window in the place; it faced the street. A dark-colored blind drawn over the window and a heavy curtain over the blind itself prevented the light from seeping through to the street.

Doran suddenly remembered that he hadn't reloaded his guns. He jerked them out hastily, crammed fresh cartridges into the chambers and holstered the Colts again. When he looked up he found the woman watching him, waiting.

"Whenever you're ready."

He hitched up his belt, and shifted his holsters a bit.

"Reckon I'm ready now."

She opened the door. He strode forward, halted on the threshold, turned and looked down at her again. She seemed older now with the light behind her.

"You'll find a shed at the end of the alley," she said. "Beyond the last stall in the shed is a door. It opens onto a path that will take you safely out of town."

He nodded understandingly.

"Swell," he said. "D'yuh mind if I ask who yuh are?"

She flushed a bit.

"No," she said slowly. "I'm Mary Donlin."

"Donlin?" he repeated. "Oh, yeah—ain't that the name o' the feller that runs the saloon down the street aways?"

"Yes," she said simply.

He stepped into the alley.

"Goodbye, Doran—and good luck."

" 'Bye, Ma'am—an' thanks."

He trudged down the alley, turned presently and looked back over his shoulder. She had stepped outside, too; she seemed very slight now in the shadowy darkness, standing there, watching him.

He turned away and strode off in the direction of the shed.

A chilling wind droned over the range. It forced Doran to snap up the collar of his jacket. After a while he buttoned it tightly around his neck. He pulled the brim of his hat down over his eyes and settled himself deeper in the saddle. He looked up quickly, questioningly, whenever he thought he heard something other than the metallic ring of the mare's pounding hoofs.

His thoughts were a confused jumble now, with faces, particularly Mary Donlin's, flashing through his mind. He wondered about her. Certainly there was some connection between her and Sears. There had to be—otherwise how would she have known about the raid on the Bar-M? He puzzled over it for a time until, failing to find an answer to the question, gave it up.

Now he began to grow a bit uneasy. If, as Mary had insisted, the raiders planned to attack at dawn, then he was increasingly certain that they had already taken up their positions surrounding the Bar-M. ...

Bess slid to a sudden halt and nearly jolted Doran out of the saddle. Taken completely unawares, he fell forward against the mare's arched neck.

"Doggone yuh," he sputtered. "Why'n heck don'tcha—"

He forced himself up again. He never finished the sentence, for his eyes strayed upward—skyward—and widened. He stared hard at what he saw, almost incredulously. The sky was aglow with a red, smoldering light—flames!

In that instant he knew that he was too late; the raiders had beaten him to the Bar-M.

Perhaps now, as he stared skyward, the raiders, having managed to set the house on fire, were rushing it. Fulfillment of their mission was almost completed. The startled, dazed occupants of the house would come stumbling out, choking and coughing in the stifling smoke; hired guns would mow them down, slaughter them as they fought to reach the safety of the open.

Then his keen ears caught an echoing thunder of faraway, crashing guns. Something about the roar of gunfire gave him strange assurance. There was defiance in the voices of these guns—they were the defenders' guns! There was still a chance, he told himself.

He drove his spurs into the mare's quivering flanks.

"Go on!" he cried.

Bess streaked away.

CHAPTER FIFTEEN

THE MYSTERY OF
MOON PASS

Bess panted to a jerky halt within the shadowy darkness of a narrow passageway between two hulking barns. There was a roar of crackling, exploding flames just beyond. Peering out, Doran beheld a mounting curtain of eager flames swirling madly around and through a low, flat building. Huge, yellow-tipped flames darted through the roof of the structure and climbed skyward, lighting up the heavens.

"Bunkhouse," Doran muttered to himself, identifying the building.

The flames held his attention for another moment—bright, meteor-like sparks that crackled and hissed shot high into the reddened sky. Doran's eyes ranged over the burning building; there was no sign of life about it, nothing but a motionless figure sprawled out in front of it, face downward in the dirt.

Directly opposite the passageway, probably fifty or sixty feet away, was the Bar-M ranchhouse—a darkened, silent, two-story building. A quick, appraising look at it told Doran that it was as yet unharmed. As he stared at it a dozen men, their upraised guns gleaming in the flame-lit night, raced past the passageway. Hastily Doran backed the mare deeper into the protective shadows. He dismounted and edged his way forward, flattening out against a towering barn wall. Cautiously he looked out.

The men had halted a dozen feet beyond him. Quickly they spread out, crouched down and faced the ranchhouse. Flame suddenly belched from their guns. Lead sprayed the front of the house, ranging upward from the front door to the very roof. As Doran watched, a curtain over a window on the upper floor was suddenly thrown back and a heavy shotgun thundered a defiant answer. A crouching man forced himself up, turned slowly, tottered and dropped his gun and crumpled up on the grass.

"Give it to 'em!" a voice roared.

The raiders' guns blazed again in unison, and bullets spattered against the darkened house like hail. A window fell in with a curious tinkle of broken glass, then another, but instantly other windows in the house came alive with flashing, thundering guns. The very ground seemed to rock. The raiders, dashing this way and that to avoid offering themselves as stationary targets, emptied their guns into the house.

"Load up an' rush 'em!" someone cried above the roar of crashing guns.

Doran jerked out one of his guns, wheeled and dashed back through the passageway. Bess turned and watched him curiously. He plunged around the side of a barn, circled the burning bunkhouse and broke into the open again. He raised his gun and snapped a couple of lightning shots in the general direction of the ranchhouse. It was purely for appearances, and while it created the desired impression upon a couple of raiders who spotted him and decided that he was one of them, it produced a totally undesired effect upon a hidden rifleman in an upper window. A bullet whined past Doran's head, uncomfortably close, too, struck a half buried rock a few feet beyond him and glanced off. Doran ducked instinctively, like a wild horse dodging a spinning lariat in the hands of a pursuing cowboy. The rifle cracked a second time, but the target that was Doran was no longer there.

He heard pounding feet behind him and shot a backward, questioning glance over his shoulder. A man was running after him. Doran slowed down deliberately.

"C'mon!" he yelled.

He went on again, this time at a slower pace. The man caught up with him, but now they were past the reflected light from the burning bunkhouse, and in the night light he was just another raider—or so he appeared to be.

"Go 'head!" the newcomer panted at Doran's heels. "Head fer the back o' the house an' mebbe we kin bust in an' rout 'em out inter the open!"

Doran made no answer. There was no need for one. Together they raced toward the house, swung around it. Doran had already shifted his gun in his hand. He spun around suddenly and clubbed the raider over the head with the heavy butt of his Colt. The man went down like a poled steer. Doran darted away again. He reached the back door of the house, tried it hopefully and cursed when it refused to open. He hammered on it with the butt of his gun.

"Bud!" he yelled. "C'mon—open 'er up!"

There was no response. He frowned and holstered his gun, backed up a bit and suddenly hurled himself at the door. It gave way before him, and the impetus of his charge sent him plunging full-tilt into the house. He collided with a chair, fell over it and sprawled out on the floor.

"Damn it!" he panted; then, in a louder and impatient voice: "Bud! Where are yuh?"

A roar of gunfire suddenly arose now and drowned him out. The defenders' guns thundered a speedy reply to the blast from the attackers. Doran climbed to his feet, wincing when he touched his left knee. He straightened up again, slowly, and, hugging the wall, made his way through the darkened room toward what he decided was a door. He stumbled a second time and halted instantly. There was something on the floor, and he nudged it with his foot. He bent down and touched it, ran his hands over it. It was a huddled body of a man.

Doran stepped over the body and groped his way forward again, bumped into a closed door and cursed under his breath, jerked open the door and found himself in a narrow, shadowy hallway. He heard footsteps overhead, then the crash of a rifle and the prompt answering thunder of guns outside the house.

He heard running feet somewhere nearby—the heavy scraping of boots on gravel. The sound grew louder, and he backed into the darkened room, retreated into a shadowy corner and waited. The back door was pushed open. His guns leaped into his hands.

"Hey!" a voice said excitedly. "What d'yuh know—the back door's open!"

"Oh, yeah—swell!" another voice promptly answered. "Awright, yuh fellers—hop inside. Reckon we got 'em now. C'mon—don't take all night about it!"

Tall, shadowy figures filled the doorway—three, four, five of them—then a sixth one.

"Darker'n all hell in here," a man mumbled, and fell over the chair just as Doran had done a few minutes before. "Damn it—ouch!"

"Why don'tcha watch where yuh're goin'?" a voice demanded gruffly. "Red, how d'yuh get upstairs?"

"Foller me," the man named Red replied. "I'll show yuh."

The raiders fell in behind him and filed across the room, past the corner in which Doran crouched. The door that opened upon the narrow hallway was swung wide.

"There yuh are," Red said. "An' there's the stairs 'gainst the wall. See 'em?"

"Nope—but I'm willin' tuh take yore word fer it that they're there."

Then still another door was flung open—this time on the landing on the upper floor. Heavy boots sounded on the upper steps.

"Look out!" a voice cried.

"Hey, what the—"

Guns suddenly roared in the hallway, and others thundered in reply. A body fell heavily, thumped and rolled down the stairs. Guns blazed again. A man cried out, another grunted as though the wind had been driven out of him, and a third cursed loudly. Boots sounded on the stairs again, someone scrambled backwards, then the upper floor door banged loudly.

"Rush 'em!"

Heavy steps echoed from the stairway; then the raiders hurled themselves against the door behind which the retreating defenders had taken refuge.

"Blast it down!"

Gunfire thundered through the house. There was a ripping, splintering sound; then it was evident that the door had finally given way before the volley of lead, for it banged loudly. Again the ear-splitting crash of guns arose. It grew in volume for a moment, then seemed to fade away completely, leaving the air strangely hushed and heavy. Booted feet scraped over the floors.

"Reckon that's that," a voice said with finality. "Let's go."

"Wait a minute, Steve—how 'bout the girl?"

"Huh? Oh, yeah—kinda fergot about her fer the minute. There's a lamp outside the door. One o' you fellers light it an' bring it in here so's we kin have a look at 'er."

Someone strode out to the head of the stairs. A minute later a light flamed on the landing; then it was withdrawn. "Shucks," the man named Steve said presently. "Ain't nuthin' much the matter with her. Look's tuh me like she just passed out in the excitement—that's all."

"Uh-huh. Go 'head, you fellers—you get the horses. I'll kinda bring 'er aroun'...."

A man laughed coarsely.

"Oh, yeah? Who're yuh tryin' tuh kid, huh?"

"Pipe down," Steve commanded. "Get goin', fellers. Hustle that girl along downstairs, Pinto. We ain't got all night, y'know."

"Shore, Steve—shore."

Heavy feet sounded on the landing, then came down the stairs. Three men made their way past Doran, filed out of the house and trudged away. Doran holstered his guns. He stepped into the hallway, but retreated almost instantly when he heard Pinto's quick step on the landing. The man came dashing down the stairs recklessly in the darkness. He whirled past Doran and plunged toward the back door which stood ajar. He slammed it shut, caught up the chair and braced it against the door, backed away from it, turned finally and strode swiftly toward the hallway.

A tall, shadowy figure came out of the darkness to meet him. Doran hurled himself at the raider. They went down together, heavily, in a tangled mass of threshing legs and swinging arms. Punches thudded against panting, twisting bodies. Now one of them broke away from the other, rolled away and scrambled to his feet. The other bounded to his feet, too.

A lean, lithe figure whirled forward. A terrific, jaw-shattering punch found its mark. A man fell back against the wall. Two heavy punches thudded home, cruelly, viciously. A body crumpled and slid sideways to the floor.

A horseman clattered up to the front of the house.

"Pinto!"

Doran turned and stumbled into the hallway. The body of a man lay at the foot of the stairs. Doran stepped over him, made his way up the stairs and pushed into a lamplit room. He halted just inside the doorway. His eyes ranged over the room. On the floor—it had once been a bedroom, although now it was a shambles, with overturned and broken furniture scattered about and curtains hanging by shreds from the windows—lay the sprawled bodies of six men. Doran's eyes sought and found Ann Miller. She lay on the floor, near the head of her bed, her hands gripping the bedclothes tightly, almost desperately, as though she had tried to pull herself up.

"Pinto!"

Doran's eyes came away from the girl. He looked up. He realized that he dared not show himself at the shattered window.

"Yeah?" he yelled gruffly, pretended annoyance in his voice.

" 'Bout time yuh answered, doggone yuh," Steve yelled back. "What'n hell's keepin' yuh? Get that girl down here pronto, y'hear? We're goin' on ahead. You foller us."

"Right," Doran answered. "I'm comin'."

Steve clattered away.

Doran made his way to the nearest window. Guardedly he peered out. He saw the other raiders ride up to meet Steve. Presently the band loped off toward McCloud.

Doran turned away from the window. He glanced at some of the huddled figures on the floor. There was something familiar about one of them. Doran started forward, hesitated, as though he had been forewarned, forced himself on again, halted beside the motionless man, bent down, and turned him over on his back.

It was Bud Watkins, and he was dead.

The limitless canopy of sky was strangely empty and colorless for a brief, hushed moment, like a vast stage without footlights and scenery; then a faint glow suddenly appeared on the horizon. It was dawn, and in a twinkling the enveloping, shadowy veil of night that had obscured the earth was whisked away.

The light was dimmed a bit, as though an unsteady, fumbling hand were experiencing some difficulty in adjusting it. The sky grew leaden. A gentle breeze droned breathlessly over the earth; then a feathery mist drifted down. Presently it turned to rain. Solid sheets of water pounded the trail. Top soil became mud that slithered about and finally overflowed and ran off wherever it found a crevice.

Despite her double burden, Bess quickened her pace. Her iron shoes rang out sharply on the stony stretches of ground and trail. She broke into a brisk run, but Doran jerked the reins and she halted reluctantly. The girl in front of Doran on the saddle was sitting up now burying her chin in the upturned collar of the poncho. A flash of lightning startled her.

"Easy, now," Doran said behind her. "It'll be over in another minute."

She shivered and quickly buttoned the collar around her neck.

"This is the Pass," she said dully. "Moon Pass."

"Uh-huh. Fargo's at one end of it an' Tonopah's at the other—right—leastways somewheres beyond McCloud?"

"Yes."

The rain seemed to slacken now. Doran glanced skyward.

"Lettin' up," he said, and swung himself out of the saddle. He stamped his feet on the ground, shifted his holsters a bit and looked up at her. "Think yuh'd kinda like tuh stretch yore legs fer a spell?"

She nodded slowly in reply. He held up his arms, and she leaned forward. He caught her under the arms and lifted her out of the saddle. Their eyes met for a moment. It was Ann who looked away. He swung her around to avoid a patch of muddy ground, carried her off the trail and put her down gently on a flat-surfaced rock.

Bess wandered off a bit. The rain had ceased now, completely. The breeze, too, had died down. The sky grew brighter; then a warm sun burst through. Together they trudged along the trail, with Ann stepping from rock to rock so as to avoid the wet, muddy ground. Bess heard them coming, halted and waited for them. Doran stopped abruptly. Ann looked at him questioningly.

"What is it?" she asked.

He bent down and squatted on his knees and stared hard at something in the mud. She heard him laugh softly. He scooped up a handful of the mud and straightened up.

"I'll be doggoned," he muttered. He raised his eyes to hers. "Got any idea why Sears was so dead set against the railroad comin' through here?"

She shook her head.

"No," she said slowly. "I've always imagined that he wanted the West to stay as it was—untouched and unspoiled."

A cold smile tugged at the corners of his mouth.

"Yuh oughta know better'n that," he said tauntingly. "Sears ain't the sentimental kind. He's smart an' cute an' he wanted folks tuh think he was willin' tuh fight tuh keep the railroad from spoilin' the scenery. But there was somethin' else behind it—somethin' that he was tryin' tuh keep fer 'imself—somethin' he didn't want anybody else tuh find out about till the Pass an' the country 'round it was his. He's willin' tuh do anythin' tuh keep the railroad outa here because the Pass is rotten with gold! There's the hull story—that's what John Sears was after!"

CHAPTER SIXTEEN
DORAN GETS REINFORCEMENTS

THEY whirled through the Pass, the mare's pounding hoofs echoing over the stony trail that wound through it. She stiffened suddenly and threw back her head and whinnied. It was a warning, and Doran recognized it as such at once. He looked up quickly. Bess needed no command from him, no sharp jerk on the reins; she slackened her pace of her own accord. Doran's right hand dropped swiftly and tightened around the worn butt of a ready Colt. Instinctively, and quite mechanically, he loosened the gun in its holster.

Some fifty feet ahead of them two dungaree-clad men, rifles in their hands, stepped out from behind a huge, white-faced boulder on the side of the trail. They eyed the approaching mare and raised their rifles. Doran grunted. His hand came away from his gun butt.

"They're awright," he said presently. "They're railroad men."

Ann had been watching them with anxious eyes.

"Oh," she said simply, and relaxed.

One of the men turned abruptly and trudged to the opposite side of the trail, halted there, turned and waited. His companion glanced at him, sauntered forward a bit and stopped. Bess pulled up directly in front of them.

"Howdy," Doran greeted them.

"Hiya," the man who had sauntered forward said. He looked sharply at Doran, at Ann, then at Doran again. "Where yuh bound fer, stranger?"

"Fer the railroad camp," Doran explained. "Reckon it's somewheres 'round here, ain't it?"

"Somewheres—yeah," the man drawled.

"Know if Jim Reynolds is there?" Doran asked.

"Who?"

"Jim Reynolds," Doran repeated. "Cap'n Jim Reynolds."

"Oh—Cap'n Reynolds, eh?" The man nodded slowly. "Yeah, he's there. Wanna see 'im?"

Doran grinned.

"Nope. Got an idea though that he wants tuh see me."

The man studied him for a moment.

"You one o' Reynolds' men?"

Doran nodded. The man relaxed. He lowered his rifle.

"Bill...."

The second man came around the mare.

"Yeah?"

"It's awright, Bill. This feller ain't one o' them hell-raisers from McCloud. He's one o' Cap'n Reynolds' hands —comp'ny police, y'know."

Bill's eyebrows arched.

"Oh, yeah?"

He shot a glance at Doran.

"Show 'im where th' camp's at, will yuh, Bill?"

"Shore," the latter replied. He slung his rifle under his arm. "Awright, Mister—foller me."

Doran drew rein in front of a crude, unpainted shack. A man with a shovel over his right shoulder trudged by, looked up curiously, hesitated a moment and finally halted and retraced his steps.

"Lookin' fer somebody?" he asked.

Doran nodded.

"Yeah—Cap'n Reynolds," he replied. He nodded toward the shack. "That his office?"

Before the man could answer, the shack's door was flung open. A tall figure appeared in the doorway. Doran grinned broadly. It was Reynolds. He frowned and stared at the mare, at the girl and the man astride the white horse.

"Howdy, Cap'n."

"Why, doggone yore ornery hide!" Reynolds exploded. He strode out. The shack's door banged loudly behind him. He halted beside the mare, his hands on his hips, and looked up at Doran. "Where'n hell 've you been, huh?"

Doran laughed lightly. Reynolds suddenly remembered the girl on the saddle in front of Doran. He looked up at her now, flushing under her steady eyes.

"Oh, excuse me, Ma'am," he said awkwardly. "Kinda fergot myself fer a minute. Been worryin' 'bout this young polecat an' wonderin' if he was 'live or dead—an' when I saw 'im sittin' up there an' grinnin' at me, reckon it was just my way o' showin' my relief. You—Dan—get down offa that horse!"

Doran swung himself out of the saddle.

"Wa-al?" Reynolds demanded impatiently. "Talk up! Whatcha gotta say fer yoreself?"

"Mind if I introduce her, first?" Doran asked with a grin, nodding toward Ann.

Captain Reynolds frowned again.

"Sent yuh up there tuh clean up a bunch o' no-good hellions," he snapped, "an' yuh get mixed up with a girl instead. Awright—let's get it over with. I'm Reynolds, Ma'am, chief o' Western Railways' police. I'm glad tuh know yuh an' I'm plumb s'prised tuh find a good-lookin' girl like you wastin' yore time on a lazy maverick like him!"

Ann stiffened in the saddle.

"Take it easy, Cap'n," Doran said hastily. "Don't go jumpin' at conclusions. This is Ann Miller."

"Awright," Reynolds grunted. "Miller—didja say? Her ol' man the rancher Matt Burnham tol' us about?"

"Ben Miller," Ann said quietly, "was my father."

The captain grunted again.

"Uh-huh," he said; then: "Hol' on a minute. What d'yuh mean *was* yore father?"

Doran flushed.

"What Miss Miller means, Cap'n," he said quietly, "is that 'er father's dead."

"No!"

Doran nodded mutely.

"Hope yuh got a line on the ornery skunk that done it, Dan?" Reynolds asked grimly.

There was a strained silence for a moment.

"Miss Miller's plumb tuckered out, Cap'n," Doran said presently. "She could do with some grub an' a bed. Figger you kin provide 'em fer 'er?"

"Shore kin!"

Reynolds turned. The man with the shovel on his shoulder was still standing there, wide-eyed and listening interestedly. The captain frowned and gave him a withering stare.

"Wa-al?" he snapped.

The man reddened and started away.

"You!" Reynolds barked.

The man jerked to a halt. He turned around slowly, hesitantly.

"Talkin' tuh me, Cap'n?" he asked almost timidly.

"Yeah—you! Run down tuh the cook's shanty an' tell 'im tuh hustle some hot grub up here!" Reynolds commanded.

"Shore, Boss—right away!"

The man lumbered away, the shovel thumping clumsily on his shoulder. Reynolds watched him for a moment, snorted and shook his head.

"Wonder if he kin make any better time when he hears the paymaster hollerin' 'is name," he mused. He turned again to

Ann. "Yuh kin use my place, Miss Miller. 'Course it ain't much fer looks an' furnishin's; still, it's clean, an' that's somethin', specially fer this neck o' the woods."

"Thank you."

"Dan!" the captain barked suddenly. "Doggone it, man — don't stan' there like yuh was a hitchin' post! Help that girl climb down offa yore horse!"

Doran stepped forward and held up his arms. She swung herself halfway out of the saddle. He caught her, lifted her clear and put her down on the ground.

"Go 'head, Ma'am," Reynolds said, nodding toward the shack. "It's all yourn. If yuh need anything, just holler."

Ann smiled wanly. The men separated to permit her to pass, but she swung wide around Reynolds and marched swiftly toward the shack. In another moment the door closed behind her. Reynolds glanced at Doran.

" 'Less I'm readin' the signs all wrong, Dan," he said quietly, "I'm willin' tuh bet yuh stepped inter somethin' way over yore head."

"An' how I did!" Doran said disgustedly. "An' if yuh think I ain't made one helluva fine mess outa things—wa-al, yuh better think again."

"Let's have it. Reckon I might's well know the worst right off."

"S'pose we kinda amble off aways," Doran suggested, "so's we kin talk in private?"

The captain shrugged his shoulders.

"Whatever yuh say, Dan."

Together they sauntered away.

The camp lay in a wide hollow with tall trees encircling it and forming a barricade between it and the outside world. In the night light the upper reaches of the trees seemed to dissolve into black nothingness. Presently, however, when the moon appeared and flooded the camp with silvery light, the trees became whole again and stood out clearly against the backdrop of brightened sky.

There were lights in most of the buildings in the camp. The long, flat building which served as the dining room was brightly lighted, more so than any of the others; through its windows and opened doors one could see aproned men hurrying about, clearing away the tables and carrying off used dishes to an adjoining shack for washing. Other men busied themselves straightening things up.

In the smaller buildings—they were little more than shacks—in which the paymaster, the doctor, and the camp's office force were housed—there was activity, too. In the bunkhouses poker games were in progress. Loud voices arose, and here and there a quick, boastful laugh was audible—the result of a winning play. From a dimly lighted shack the strains of a song—a man's voice and a strumming guitar—floated out through a half opened door.

Small bands of men, some of them with rifles over their shoulders, others with their rifles slung under their arms, marched out of camp and disappeared into the night. They were the men who had been ordered to stand guard in and out around the Pass, evidence of a wholesome respect for the night riders from McCloud. Minutes after they disappeared other men, similarly armed, trudged wearily into camp. Now that they were relieved, they seemed possessed of but one desire—hot food—and they headed straight for the dining room.

Some of the poker games broke up and the players filed out and lounged in front of the bunkhouses. It was something of a ritual. Some idle talk, a last cigarette, a hasty, mechanical glance at the sky, and they were ready to turn in. One by one they made their way back inside and stretched out in their bunks. There was some shortlived clowning and banter, but the lights went out presently. Tired men dozed off quickly.

Doran sauntered along the "street." He had been away all afternoon. He had missed Reynolds at supper, and he wondered if the grizzled lawman had gone to his shack to make certain that Ann had been taken care of. He came abreast of the shack. The door opened and a slim figure—Ann Miller's—filled the doorway. He halted and touched his hat.

"Even'," he said. "Yuh seen the cap'n?"

"No," Ann replied.

He came a bit closer.

"Rode over tuh yore place this afternoon," he began casually.

"Did you?"

"Went over on account o' young Watkins," he continued. "Couldn't just leave 'im there, y'know—like he was."

There was no response, no comment.

"He was a swell kid, awright."

"You—you buried him?" she asked.

He nodded slowly, then was silent for a moment.

"Miss Ann," he began again presently, "there's somethin' I'd like tuh tell yuh. I s'ppose I oughta let yuh try tuh ferget it stead o' remindin' yuh of it again; still there's no tellin' when I'll get another chance tuh talk tuh yuh like this. D'yuh mind listenin', if I promise tuh make it short's I kin?"

"Go on."

He drew a deep breath.

"Wa-al, the first day I hit town Sears offered me a job. 'Course he didn't have no idea who I was or that I was workin' fer the railroad. As a matter o' fact I even told 'im I was on the dodge fer killin' a feller, so it ain't s'prisin' that he got the idea that I was willin' tuh do some more killin' long's I got paid fer doin' it."

"You wanted him to think that?"

"Shore. Y'see, I got the fool idea that by workin' fer somebody like Sears, I'd be on the inside o' things. I figgered it'd be a cinch fer me then tuh find out what was goin' on, who was doin' it an' why. Then, soon's I got on tuh things, shucks, I could bust 'em up," he explained. "On'y trouble was, things didn't work out the way I expected 'em to."

He paused again.

"Wa-al," he went on, "I got th' job awright. That's how I come tuh ride with Sears' men that night—the night o' the raid, y'know. Sears didn't tell me much 'bout what I was s'pposed tuh do. 'Course I knew there was gonna be some killin' tuh be done, but I figgered by the time I came tuh that I'd be able tuh stall it off. Anyway, that first night he told me tuh ride out an' meet Foster an' some o' his men. It was when I met 'em that I found out that we were gonna raid the Bar-M.

"Wa-al, yuh know what happened. Yuh kin take my word fer this—I never aimed at any o' the Bar-M riders. Oh, I was doin' plenty o' shootin', awright—goin' through the motions, y'understand, tuh make Foster think I was the kind o' killer Sears thought he'd hired—but I was shootin' over their heads. Anyway, we got surrounded —Foster an' me—an' then tuh top it all off, I got plugged. Yore Dad an' his men were closin' in on us fast. We hadda get away. I raised my gun tuh shoot at their horses. Somebody bumped inter me, my gun went off, an' that's all I kin remember. I didn't even see yore Dad fall offa his horse."

She was silent and rigid. In the shadowy darkness he could see nothing of her face.

" 'Course I'm doggoned sorry 'bout what happened, but I know danged wall that bein' sorry ain't enough tuh bring yore Dad back tuh life. On'y reason I had fer wantin' tuh tell yuh the hull story was—wa-al, I wanted yuh tuh hear it direct from me. Besides, Miss Ann, I wanted yuh tuh know how rotten I felt 'bout it."

He paused and moistened his lips.

"Bud saved my life," he went on, "an' that night in the shack I reckon I'da died if you hadn'ta come along an' tended to me. There's nuthin' I kin do fer Bud now —he's dead—'cept of course square things up fer 'im with the hellions who killed 'im. That much I aim tuh do an' pronto. As fer you, Miss Ann—I dunno how I'm ever gonna repay yuh 'less yuh gimme a chance an' — wa-al, mebbe somethin'll come up an'—"

From the darkened Pass came the echoing clatter of pounding hoofs. Doran's voice faded away. He looked up quickly. A shadowy horseman came whirling into view at the head of the single street that ran the length of the camp. The horseman pulled up in front of the shack. His mount slid to a stiff-legged, dust-raising halt.

"Dan!" the man cried. "That you standin' there?"

It was Reynolds' voice. Doran wheeled and strode over to him.

"What's the matter, Cap'n?" he asked. "Where yuh been?"

Reynolds laughed lightly.

"Oh, places," he replied. "Got a hankerin' tuh see what McCloud was like, so I went a-visitin'."

"Oh, yeah?"

"Got a lead tuh foller, Dan. Mebbe it's worth lookin' into. I'll tell yuh 'bout it later on. Meantime, go get yore horse, boy—we're ridin'."

"Awright—but where are we goin'?"

The captain laughed again.

"We're gonna do some grave-diggin', Dan. We're gonna be diff'rent 'bout it, though—we're gonna dig up a feller 'stead o' plantin' one! Get yore horse an' make it lively!"

CHAPTER SEVENTEEN
THE DEAD BEAR WITNESS

THE moon that had been bright and silvery but minutes before now slipped behind a bank of billowing clouds. The earth was again plunged into darkness. Things lost shape and became blurred or faded away into nothingness. Tall trees that were erect and clearly outlined against the blue sky were now lost in the night light.

A cool, chilling wind raced inland from the river and droned through the grass and brush. Here and there trees swayed in the wake of the fleeting wind; they made one think of a great hand being waved backwards and forwards over the shadowy earth. One heard the moan of the wind a moment later in the short-cropped grass on the range beyond.

Strangely, too, there was no sign now of the river. In the moonlight it had gleamed like a silvery ribbon—in the darkness it disappeared, faded from sight. There was no sound from the direction of the river—nothing but a momentary and almost feather-like murmur of the current or the whispered wash of the water on the river's banks. The far-spreading range that began at the very edge of the river was dark and silent and mysterious.

The Bar-M ranchhouse was a solid block of shadowy darkness, gloomily dark and oppressively hushed. The three horses that had pulled up in front of it seemed nervous and uneasy in the silence of the night. They appeared to sense the fact that the heavy hand of death lay on the place. They stole glances at the house as though they knew that dead men lay within. They whinnied softly, timidly, like a small child whimpering because the enveloping darkness frightened him, and pawed the ground nervously, then impatiently. The chill wind made them even more restless, and they milled about, huddling against one another and refusing to stand still. The saddles on their backs creaked beneath the shifting weight of their riders.

Opposite the ranchhouse were the thick barns—huge squares of blackness that loomed up even larger than they actually were—an illusion caused by the confusing night light.

Midway between the house and the barns was a curious, fire-blackened stretch of ground—the site of the burned bunkhouse.

On the scorched earth in front of the wind-blown embers lay a single outstretched figure face downward in the dirt, motionless in death. In the grass in front of one of the bulky barns were two more dead men—raiders.

"Gloomy as hell," Reynolds muttered, "ain't it?"

"Shore is," Doran answered.

The third horseman edged his mount in between the captain's horse and Bess.

"Captain Reynolds—" he began.

The lawman turned slightly in his saddle.

"Doggone it, Doc," he said reproachfully, "you ain't gonna start beefin' again, are yuh?"

"I'm sorry," the man said stiffly, "but I still don't see why you routed me up out of bed and insisted that I accompany you here. You don't need a doctor here, certainly not a railroad doctor—you should have brought along a ghost breaker. I must insist—"

"Now, Doc—"

"I must insist that you take me back to camp at once," the man concluded.

Reynolds grunted an indistinct reply. He swung around toward Doran.

"Dan."

"Yeah?"

"Where'bouts is that Miller feller buried?"

"Miller?" Doran repeated in surprise. "Yuh mean Ben Miller—Ann's father?"

" 'Course," the captain snapped.

"What's the idea? What d'yuh want o' him?"

"You'd be s'prised," Reynolds said grimly.

"Reckon I would," Doran said. "He's buried down near the river."

Reynolds straightened up in the saddle.

"Awright then. You lead the way. Me an' Doc'll trail along behind yuh. Oh, yeah, Dan—yuh got them shovels I gave yuh?"

"Huh? Shovels?" Doran repeated. Then he remembered the two shovels the captain had given him; he had lashed them to his saddle and promptly forgotten about them. "Oh, shore—I got 'em."

"Then go 'head."

Doran was motionless for another moment. He was recalling what Reynolds had said to him earlier ... "We're gonna dig up a feller 'stead o' plantin' one!"

Obviously it was Ben Miller who was to be "dug up" —but why?

He eyed Reynolds sharply, questioningly, but in the night light the captain's face was expressionless. He wondered what was behind the idea; wondered if—

"Wa-al, Dan?" Reynolds growled impatiently. "Whatcha waitin' fer? It's gettin' late, y'know. Ain't no sense in lettin' this bus'ness take any longer'n it has to."

Doran nudged Bess with his knees. The jittery mare, eager to be off again, bounded away almost instantly. Doran jerked the reins sharply and checked her.

"Awright, Doc," he heard Reynolds say presently. "Foller Doran. I'll bring up the rear so's no ghost kin reach out an' carry yuh off without me seein' 'em."

The doctor answered, but indistinctly.

It was probably some two hours later when three wearied men trudged back to where their tethered horses huddled together and mounted them; then, with Doran again leading the way and Doctor White and Captain Reynolds following close behind him, they rode slowly up the trail from the river's edge. They made their way through the dark, narrow passageway between the two hulking barns, emerged presently into the brighter light and halted on the grassy square of ground that lay between the house and the barns.

Conscious of it and unable to resist the impulse, they found themselves turning to look at the silent house as though some hidden but compelling force drew their eyes to it.

Reynolds broke the spell first. He jerked his mount around and pulled him up alongside the doctor's horse.

"Wa-al, Doc?" he asked. "What d'yuh say?"

The latter shrugged his shoulders.

"What would you like me to say?" he countered. "Actually, all I can do is repeat what I told you before. Miller, or whatever that man's name was, did not die of that bullet wound. The bullet struck him high up in the fleshy part of his shoulder—much too high up to have caused his death."

"Uh-huh," the captain nodded. "Then what did he die of?"

"It's my opinion that his heart gave way," the doctor replied. "I might even add that it is my belief that he was quite dead even before the bullet struck him. The force of the fired shot is what tumbled him out of his saddle."

"Yuh hear that, Dan?" Reynolds asked, turning toward Doran.

The latter edged his horse forward.

"Doc," he began. "Them there flares we lit weren't all they shoulda been. If yuh missed anything in that lousy light, nobody kin say the fault was all yourn."

"Really?" the doctor said coldly.

Doran disregarded the man's biting tone.

"Yuh couldn'ta got more'n just a look at 'im," he went on. "Right? Wa-al, don'tcha think yuh oughta hold off passin' final judgment on what he died from till yuh have another look at 'im—say in the daylight? It might prove kinda embarrassin' to yuh later on tuh say one thing tuh night an' hafta say somethin' else tomorrer."

"Why, doggone yuh, Dan—"

"Take it easy, Cap'n," Doran said calmly. "It ain't that I'm tryin' tuh make out that the doc don't know his bus'ness. Even though I'm a heap more concerned 'bout how Miller died than either o' you two fellers are, I'm big enough tuh wait fer the doc tuh have another look at him if he's got even the tiniest kind of a doubt. I just want 'im tuh be sure—that's all."

"Heck, Dan," Reynolds said quickly. "The doc knows what tuh look fer when he sees a dead man. He knows what kin kill yuh, an' what can't. Some doctors hafta examine yuh from sunup tuh sundown before they kin tell yuh what ails yuh. Others kin tell yuh right off without no fussin' aroun'. Anyway, Doc White's told yuh what he thinks. What more d'yuh want 'im tuh do?"

"Nuthin'," Doran said calmly. "If what he's said a'ready is final, then I reckon that's all there is to it."

"I'll stand by what I said before," the doctor said sharply. "Miller died of natural causes—that's absolutely final."

"There y'are, boy!" Reynolds said heartily.

"That's swell," Doran said with a grin. "Much obliged, Doc. Reckon that leaves me in the clear. Long's my bullet didn't kill Ben Miller, I'm plumb satisfied."

Moon Pass was dark and silent. They rode through it slowly, in single file, with Captain Reynolds in the lead this time and Doctor White and Doran riding behind him, each silent, each apparently busy with his own thoughts.

It was Doran who looked up suddenly, spurred Bess and overtook Reynolds and pulled up beside him.

"Cap'n," Doran said quickly, "notice anythin' aroun' here? Anythin' missin', I mean?"

The captain laughed lightly.

"Nope," he answered. "Everythin' looks 'bout the same tuh me. Long's the Pass is still here, reckon everythin' else is, too."

"Oh, yeah?" Doran retorted. "Look again, Cap'n; then mebbe yuh kin tell me what's become o' the guards."

"Huh? The guards?" Reynolds echoed.

"Yeah. They're s'pposed tuh be out here, ain't they?" Doran demanded.

The captain's horse slid to a sudden, stiff-legged halt.

"Doggone," Reynolds muttered. "Doggoned if you ain't got somethin' there, Dan. Now where'n hell d'yuh s'ppose they're at?"

"S'ppose you tell me?"

Reynolds' eyes ranged over the trail ahead of them. He shook his head slowly, thoughtfully.

"Can't, Dan," he said. He tightened his grip on the reins. "We'll find out, though, pronto! C'mon, boy—let's go!"

Their horses bounded away, their pounding hoofs echoing sharply through the shadow-drenched Pass. The doctor looked up suddenly in surprise. Not to be outdone, he spurred his horse and sent him clattering away in pursuit. Bess was whirling, racing over the stony trail with lightning, flashing hoofs. The captain's horse strove mightily to keep pace with her, but his efforts were futile. There was no overtaking the mare, no catching up with her, for, given her head and a free rein, Bess swept over the ground like a frightened deer. She literally ran Reynolds' horse into the ground. But the captain was a diehard; he cursed and lashed his mount and drove him on, pounding over the stone and turf, unwilling to let Bess make a runaway of things. Thundering hoofs drum-rolled through the shadowy Pass.

The doctor's horse never had a chance. The other two horses simply ran away from him, and he dropped behind, so far behind them that actual pursuit was quickly abandoned.

Doran, preparing himself for instant action, loosened his guns in their holsters. He had already decided that something had happened; he realized that it must have been something of a serious nature, else the guards would not have abandoned their posts.

Then with startling suddenness a roar of gunfire broke the hushed silence of the night. The outburst came from the direction of the railroad camp.

"Dan!" Reynolds cried. "Pull up!"

Doran twisted around in his saddle.

"Pull up!" the captain cried again.

Doran's hands tightened on the reins. Bess, snorting and panting, fought wildly for her head, but her master's strong arms jerked her to a side-heaving stop. Reynolds' horse came thundering up.

"Gunfire!" the captain cried. "Did yuh hear it?"

" 'Course."

"What d'yuh make of it?"

"Dunno," Doran replied, " 'less it's 'nother one o' Sears' s'prise raids. He goes in fer 'em y'know, in a big way."

"Uh-huh. Wa-al, whatever it is, there ain't any sense in our bustin' in on it. We'd better take it easy an' kinda edge our way inter the party so's we kin see what's goin' on."

"Awright. S'ppose we go on till we reach the wagon road that leads down inter camp, leave our horses there an' work our way in on foot?"

Reynolds grunted.

"Sounds sensible tuh me. Go 'head!"

Doran wheeled Bess around, spurred her and sent her dashing away again. The captain's horse was ready for her this time; he darted after, caught up with her and clung doggedly to her flying heels. Then they were racing downhill; another minute and they were out of the Pass. The trail swung away sharply toward the west; a steep, uneven, rutted road broke into the trail. It was the wagon road. At its base lay the camp. The horses were pulled up abruptly. Doran slid out of the saddle. A whack of his open hand on the mare's rump sent her loping into a nearby thicket and out of sight.

"Over here, Cap'n!"

Reynolds dismounted. Doran leaped to his side. He swung the captain's horse around, headed him toward the thicket and raised his hand as he had done to Bess, but the horse shied away, bounded past him and went plunging into the thicket. A whinny from Bess guided him onward.

"C'mon."

Both men jerked out their guns. They dashed down the road, keeping their feet somehow, miraculously, in view of the deep ruts and the half buried rocks. Then the road levelled off and widened into the camp's single street. They panted to a momentary halt.

Gun flashes burst in front of them. A score of horsemen, shadowy and unrecognizable in the dim light, whirled up and down the darkened street, wheeling this way, then that way, and pausing only for a brief second to blast away at some equally darkened shack from whose shattered window or doorway came an answering hail of gunfire. A horse reared up on its hind legs and crashed over backwards. Its rider rolled out of the way and fought his way to his feet, wheeled, gun in hand, and blazed away at a hidden rifleman. The raider stumbled and plunged toward a shack when a withering crash of fire blasted him into a limp heap in the gutter.

"Head fer yore shack!" Doran cried. "Gotta see that the girl's awright!"

Together they plunged down the street. Two horsemen wheeled to meet them. Doran's big Colts thundered defiantly. A man sagged and fell forward in his saddle and finally slid limply to the ground. He landed on his shoulder and crashed over. His companion, evidently badly hit, seemed to wilt and crumple; he braced himself somehow, forced himself upright again with a last surge of strength, and was slowly raising his gun when another bullet from a death-dealing Colt ploughed into him and fairly tore him out of his saddle and hurled him to the ground.

Doran reached the shack a stride or two ahead of Captain Reynolds. The door was slightly ajar. It flew open when Doran's shoulder struck it, and banged loudly against something inside the shack, a something that later proved to be a broken chair. Doran went plunging in. Reynolds lumbered in, too, just behind him, and collided with him in the darkness.

"Ann!" Doran cried. "Yuh here?"

There was no reply, and had there been one it was doubtful if they would have heard it, for a sudden, furious roar of gunfire broke out anew along the smoke-filled street.

"They've got 'er!" Doran cried. "Them hellions fin'lly got 'er."

"Mebbe she's on'y hidin' somewheres, Dan? Mebbe—"

"Mebbe, hell. They got her awright, an' like's not they're probably on their way back tuh McCloud right now with 'er while we're standin' here gabbin'!"

"Then what are we waitin' fer?"

They wheeled in the darkness and dashed out. A single horseman spied them and raced after them.

"Look out, Dan!"

Reynolds cried his warning over his shoulder, swung around and fired. The onrushing horse screamed with pain, faltered and stumbled and suddenly plunged to his knees, hurling his rider over his head. Reynolds lowered his gun, and his negligence almost proved fatal. For instead of taking a clumsy and painful fall, the man landed on his hands and knees and in another moment was erect again. His guns flamed, and a bullet tore past Reynolds' head with an ominous hiss.

Fortunately, there was Doran still to be reckoned with. More alert than the grizzled captain, he sized up the situation at a glance. The raider's gun snapped upward, a second shot ripped toward Reynolds—but this time there was no target. Doran hurled himself at the captain, knocking him off his feet and out of harm's way. Then like a cat Doran whirled—his big Colts thundered mightily. There was no withstanding their power, no disputing their authority.

The man was simply blasted away—riddled and dead before he struck the ground.

CHAPTER EIGHTEEN
GUNS OF VENGEANCE

DAWN over the range!

A faint glow in the colorless sky, a warm glow that heralded the approach of day—the lifting of the veil of night.

Trees, rocks, foothills, the river in the distance—everything earthly was suddenly clear and recognizable in the brightening light of early day. Then dawn was gone. It was day.

Doran and Captain Reynolds halted just outside McCloud. Before them a strangely empty and deserted street spread away.

"Wa-al, son?"

"I'm goin' in."

"Yeah—reckon yuh'll hafta. Don't look like they're gonna bring the girl out here tuh yuh. What d'yuh want tuh do?"

Doran smiled fleetingly.

"Thanks fer askin', Cap'n," he said, "an' fer keepin' outa this. Shoulda knowed yuh'd understan' that this was kinda personal—b'tween Sears an' me. You stay here, will yuh, till I get 'bout halfway down the street?"

"An' then?"

"Wa-al, if you was tuh kinda amble along then, say as far's Donlin's, an' wait in front o' his place, reckon that'd be just about right," Doran replied.

Reynolds nodded understandingly.

"Want me tuh keep yuh covered from there on, eh?" he asked.

"Right. Long's I know nobody kin come up behind me, reckon that'll make things a heap easier."

"Shore."

Doran loosened the big Colts in their holsters. He shifted them the barest bit so that their butts were just beneath his fingers. Reynolds watched him quietly. A question framed itself in his eyes. Doran noted it.

"Loaded 'em again when we were comin' up the grade back aways," he said simply.

"Oh."

"I'm goin'."

"Awright, Dan—go 'head, on'y watch yoreself an' don't give any o' them a break. Shoot first—tuh kill."

"You bet."

"I'll be waitin' fer yuh."

Doran did not reply; there appeared to be no need for a reply. He dropped the reins on the horn of his saddle, leaving his hands free for other purposes.

"Awright, Bess."

The mare loped away. Reynolds followed them with anxious eyes, standing up in his stirrups and running his eyes over the stretch of deserted street that lay ahead of Doran. He settled himself in his saddle presently and waited impatiently, for it seemed an eternity before Doran reached the halfway mark. Then Doran was riding past Donlin's. Reynolds jerked the reins and rode slowly into town. He watched Doran. The younger man appeared relaxed in his saddle; however, the captain knew that, despite his outward nonchalance, he was ready for instant action—knew too that he was carefully scanning every window and doorway along the street.

Reynolds pulled up in front of Donlin's. He noted with surprise, at first glance, that the door was open; a second glance revealed a bulky figure just inside the place, within the shadows. It was Donlin. The saloon-keeper sauntered out and nodded to Reynolds.

"Mornin'," he said. He jerked his head in the direction of Doran. "He goin' after Sears now?"

Reynolds nodded mutely.

"Figger he kin handle the three o' them?"

Reynolds nodded again.

Unconsciously both men turned to follow Doran with their eyes. They saw him turn his head a bit and glance at the jail as he came abreast of it; they looked past him and caught their breath sharply when they saw two men suddenly emerge from the very building toward which he was headed. But both were almost instantly relieved; when the mare halted abruptly they knew at once that Doran had seen the men, too.

The latter started up the street at a brisk pace, only to halt in their tracks when they looked up and found Doran, motionless on the sleek white mare, looking over at them.

The two men appeared to exchange glances—Reynolds even thought that one of them said something out of the corner of his mouth to the other. Both suddenly backed toward the door of the building—both went for their guns at the same time. There was an equally sudden roar of gunfire. It was over in an instant—then came the usual hushed and oppressively heavy silence that always follows an outburst.

One man dropped his gun, turned slowly, stumbled and fell against the door. He slid to his knees and toppled over sideways. His hat fell off and rolled across the narrow sidewalk and came to a stop within inches of the curb.

His companion appeared to be experiencing some difficulty—he managed to get his gun out of its holster and slowly raised it. The muzzle came upward, until it seemed to be gaping at Doran; then, strangely, his arm came down again as slowly as before. His fingers opened and his gun slid out of his hand and fell to the sidewalk. He swayed a bit, but only for a moment, stared downward at the gun that lay at his feet, sagged and suddenly went down on his hands and knees. He huddled on the ground for a moment or two, his head down; then, with a tremendous effort, he forced himself up again, slowly, painfully, inch by inch, until he was erect, and braced himself on quivering, widespread legs. He stumbled across the sidewalk drunkenly, perhaps unseeing, nearly lost his balance when he reached the curb, but managed somehow to steady himself and straightened up again. Then with surprising suddenness he stiffened and pitched forward into the gutter on his face.

"God!" Donlin whispered in an awed voice.

There was no comment from Reynolds—nothing but a deep sigh of relief.

"Got 'em both," Donlin muttered, almost unbelievingly, and shook his head.

A man came dashing out of a building almost directly opposite Donlin's. Reynolds, on the alert, fired from the hip. A bullet whined past the man's head protestingly and brought him to an immediate halt.

"Hey!" he sputtered. "What in hell's—"

"Go back inside where yuh belong," the captain said curtly, "an' stay there."

The man frowned, mumbled something, turned slowly and plodded back inside the building. Reynolds grunted and lowered his gun.

Doran guided the mare to the curb and dismounted. He glanced at the motionless figure in the gutter, shifted his holsters a bit so that the butts of his guns were directly below the tips of his fingers, hitched up his belt and sauntered forward toward the door. He glanced upward at Sears' window. There was a sudden, startling shattering of the window pane, and bits of glass fell to the sidewalk. The muzzle of a rifle appeared in the broken window. Doran leaped across the intervening space toward the door. The rifle roared. Doran hurdled the sprawled body in front of the door, threw open the door and darted inside.

He heard a door slam upstairs. He whipped out his guns and stepped into the hallway and looked up. His eyes probed the shadows. There was no one on the landing. Slowly he made his way upstairs. The warped stairs creaked beneath him; then he was on the landing. He halted, looked about him and slowly backed into a corner; the wall jutted out sufficiently to provide protection for him.

A Colt roared suddenly, with a terrific burst of thunder that rocked the building. A bullet splintered the upper panel, and a thin ray of sunlight sifted through the gap and danced over the far wall of the landing. A third bullet smashed the lock, the fourth broke the upper hinge on the door, and the last one shattered the lower hinge. There was a momentary pause—silence—then the door fell outward with a deafening crash that raised a thick cloud of dust. Doran turned his head away, for the dust was stifling. He suddenly remembered his empty gun; defying the dust, he "broke" the gun and hastily crammed fresh cartridges into its chambers. He turned around again presently, shielding his eyes with an upraised arm; then the dust began to settle. He slipped out of the corner, both of his guns in his hands now, both raised and ready for the final reckoning for which he had come.

"Sears," he called.

There was no answer. He could see into the office—that is, the portion of the room that was directly in front of him. The raised blind over the paneless window permitted the brightening early morning sun to stream into the office unhampered and flood the room with dazzling light. There was no one within range of his eyes. It was the section of the office that lay to the right of the doorway that demanded caution and wariness. It was in that part of the room that Sears' desk stood; there, too, the three men would be found awaiting him.

"Awright, you hombres," he called. "All of yuh—throw out yore guns. If yuh don't, I'm comin' in after 'em, an I'll come a-shootin'."

There was a momentary pause; then a burly figure of a man—Foster—whirled into the open doorway. His upraised gun flamed twice at a shadow that appeared to be a man standing against the wall that faced the office. But the shadow was only a shadow—Doran was a foot beyond it.

A Colt boomed a deep-throated reply. Foster grunted loudly, dropped his gun and clutched at his chest. Blood stained his shirt-front; he looked down at it, drew one hand away, and seemed surprised to find blood on his fingers. He sagged against the doorjamb and stumbled out, swayed a moment on buckling legs arid fell to his knees. His lips moved, but there was no sound from him —nothing but a sigh. Then he toppled over in a limp heap.

Doran flashed past him, kicked Foster's gun out of the way and went plunging into the sunlit office. He caught a glimpse of but one other man—John Sears—seated at his desk. There was no sign of Ike Boone.

"Wa-al, Sears," he began, "reckon this is the end o' the trail fer yuh. Yore schemin' an' double-dealin' days are 'bout over."

There was no reply from the county attorney. His eyes burned fiercely in his thin and now bluish-white face.

"If yuh got anything worth sayin', reckon now's the time tuh say it."

Sears was silent. Doran shrugged his shoulders.

"Awright, Mister—get up outa there."

Sears unbuttoned his coat. He pushed his chair back from the desk and climbed slowly to his feet. His right hand crept upward, halted when it reached the lapel of his coat and suddenly darted inside toward a bulge near his left shoulder. Blue flame burst from his coat and a bullet whined past Doran's head and buried itself in the wall behind him. The Colt in Doran's right hand leaped upward and thundered deafeningly. Sears gasped, as though the breath had been driven out of his body. He withdrew his hand slowly; when it reappeared he was gripping a small, blue steel gun. He raised it, and had levelled it when the Colt roared again in protest. Sears winced and dropped his gun, which fell on the desk. He reached for it painfully, brushed it clumsily, and it slid off the desk to the floor.

He bent over and managed somehow to pick it up, straightened up again and raised it when a shudder ran through him. The gun came down again; he dropped it a second time, and this time it fell to the floor. His eyes closed gently. He tottered and fell forward over his desk.

Doran turned away. His eyes ranged over the room, over the file cabinets in one corner of the office, shifted and lighted upon the clothes closet in the opposite corner. He holstered his guns and sauntered over and jerked open the double doors. The closet was empty; a narrow panel in the back of it caught his eyes. There was nothing different about it, nothing unusual about it; still he touched it idly with one finger. Perhaps it was his curiosity that caused him to rap on it with his knuckles.

He seemed surprised at the hollow ring, frowned, and suddenly pushed against the panel. It flew open. Doran's eyes widened. He found himself staring hard, for on the other side of the panel was a tiny, windowless room. Standing against the far wall of the room was a girl, her hand pressed tightly against her lips to stifle the cry of fear that arose in her throat.

"Ann," he said quickly.

A sob escaped her.

He was over the threshold and into the room in a single stride. She stumbled toward him blindly, and he caught her in his arms.

"It's awright, Ann," he heard himself say. "It's awright now. There ain't nobody gonna bother yuh again."

She sobbed against his broad chest, and he found himself patting her back clumsily but gently. Her tears stained the front of his shirt, but he gloried in it.

"It's awright, Ann," he repeated. "There ain't anythin' tuh be scared of now. But if cryin' 'll help yuh, go 'head, honey. Yuh kin cry all yuh want to. Nobody's gonna stop yuh."

His arms tightened around her.

Doran came out of the building with Ann Miller at his side. He looked up the street and halted in his tracks.

"What in time—" he began.

"What is it?" Ann asked quickly.

He laughed lightly, reassuringly, and pointed.

"Reckon that must be the latest thing in cavalry," he said, and laughed again.

The street was alive with horsemen—the strangest-looking troop of mounted men he had ever seen. They were railroad men—more at home on the ground than they were on horse-back—and they showed it. But what they lacked in horseman-ship and ease in the saddle they made up for in grimness and determination. There were fully a hundred of them, brawny, thick-armed laborers, all of them armed either with rifles or shotguns, all of them clad in soiled and in many cases over-sized overalls.

They were stationed along the curb on both sides of the street, with a five-or six-foot interval between horsemen, their guns raised threateningly and covering the 'citizens' of the town, who appeared to be completely cowed. From the way the town's gentry stood on the sidewalks with upraised hands it was obvi-ous that they were more than casually impressed with the "cav-alry." None of them, it appeared, had dared dispute the order to stand where they were and "hoist 'em."

Doran grinned at the sight.

Two horsemen came loping down the street. One of them was Captain Reynolds; the other—Doran looked hard at the man for a moment before he recognized him. He was short and pudgy and red-faced—Matt Burnham, the President of Western Railways.

Reynolds caught sight of Doran, shouted to him, spurred his mount and came clattering up to the curb where Doran and Ann were standing. Burnham pounded up behind him. The captain slid out of the saddle.

"Dan!" he cried delightedly. He caught Doran by the arms. "Yuh son of a gun—yuh awright?"

"Shore."

"Got both o' them hellions, eh?" Reynolds asked eagerly.

Doran nodded.

"Yep, but how'd you know there was on'y two o' them?" he. demanded. "How'd you know Boone wasn't there?"

Burnham had already dismounted. He shoved Reynolds aside and halted in front of Doran and looked up at him.

"How, eh?" he echoed. "How d'yuh s'ppose he knew? Why, doggone yuh, I told 'im, that's how! That mangy sheriff was at the head o' them critters that were tryin' tuh wipe out my camp. Wa-al, soon's I got one look at Boone I knew there was one feller I could lick. I lit out after 'im, chased 'im clear down tuh the river an' booted 'im in. Hell, if I'd a knowed my strength, I'm dog-goned if I wouldn'ta gone after Sears an' Foster, too, an' polished them off along with Boone—'stead o' callin' on you fellers for help."

Reynolds laughed. He caught Doran's eye and winked.

"Show Dan what yuh took offa Boone," he suggested to Burnham.

The latter produced a silver star and held it aloft.

"There y'are—it says 'sheriff,' don't it?" He polished it by rubbing it on his shirt front. "Reckon that proves I done what I said."

Doran turned to Reynolds.

"What about the raiders?" he asked. "They get away?"

Matt Burnham snorted.

"Like hell they did," he said loudly, indignantly. "The idea! The fellers in camp drove 'em out. I come along with a hull new bunch o' men I'd hired an' we kinda caught Boone an' his pole-cats in between us an' crushed 'em. Sheriff's the on'y one that got away with a hull skin, an' if he can't swim any better'n he kin fight, reckon the fish in the river'll soon be nibblin' on his fat carcass."

"Then I reckon that's that," Doran said. "Looks like yuh oughta have clear sailin', Boss, from now on."

Burnham grunted.

"Matt tells me McCloud's gotta go," Reynolds said.

"What d'yuh mean—gotta go?"

"Wa-al, it seems like the gov'nor's fed up with complaints 'bout McCloud," Reynolds continued. "So he's told Matt tuh raze the place an' run his tracks through it."

"On the level?"

" 'Course," Burnham snapped. "We're gonna wipe this hell-hole right offa the map, an' do it so complete that nobody'll be able tuh remember that there ever was such a place as McCloud."

CHAPTER NINETEEN
TRAIL'S END

DONLIN's heart beat a bit faster when heard a quick step inside the drab shack. It was his wife's step. He had never forgotten it; he was certain he would always be able to recognize it. Then the door was being unlatched and opened. He looked up quickly, a bit flustered, and whipped off his hat. He managed a smile.

" 'Lo, Mary."

"Why, Pat!" he heard her say. Her voice hadn't changed much—there was still warmth and friendliness in it, although he thought it lacked some of its buoyancy. "How nice of you to come! Do come inside."

"Oh—thanks."

He closed the door behind him. He was careful not to let it slam. He remembered that slammed doors used to startle her. She hadn't changed much, he told himself. Of course the light wasn't very good. The blind over the window that faced the street was drawn full length, and it was difficult to tell very much. Still, he was grateful for the shadowy light, for he felt awkward and uneasy and he was glad that she couldn't see him very well either. He cleared his throat.

"Uh, Mary—"

"Yes?"

"Mary," he began again, "I got somethin' t' tell yuh. I hate tuh hafta do it, 'cause it's gonna hurt yuh. Still I kinda figgered yuh'd rather have me do the tellin' 'stead o' leaving' it tuh somebody else. It's about John."

"You've come to tell me that—that he's dead, haven't you, Pat?" she asked quietly.

His eyes widened with surprise.

"You're wondering how I knew," she went on calmly. "I didn't know—really. The shooting woke me. I had the strangest feeling, Pat—a premonition. When I saw you I knew. Was it Doran who did it?"

He nodded. He fumbled with his hat, turning it around and around in his hands. He spied a smudge on the rolled brim, scowled darkly and rubbed it vigorously with his shirt sleeve. He kept his eyes lowered, waiting for her to continue, but she was silent now. He jerked his head up finally.

"Mary," he began anew, "McCloud's gonna be torn down. The railroad's comin' through. Yuh'll hafta leave same's everybody else. Yuh're gonna hafta have some place tuh go tuh—some place where yuh'll be taken care of, y'know."

She turned slowly, made her way to the window and raised the blind part way. The bright morning sunlight poured into the shack; it scampered over the walls and the ceiling, danced lightly over the carpetless floor.

" 'Course the saloon's done fer. I ain't sorry. I've made plenty out of 'er, an' now I'm glad tuh be rid of 'er. I've bought me somethin' else, Mary—somethin' I know yuh're gonna like same's I do. Remember the Andrews' place, on the other side o' the Pass from the Bar-M? It's mine now, an' it's all paid fer, too. I've had the house fixed up an' everythin'—even got curtains, too, waitin' fer you tuh—"

He stopped abruptly. Her head was bowed now. He thought he detected a stifled sob. He swallowed hard, moistened his lips and went on again.

"We allus useter talk 'bout ownin' our own place—remember, Mary? Wa-al, we got us one now, awright—an' it's swell."

Her shoulders heaved slightly. He drew closer to her.

" 'Course I ain't the man that John Sears was. He was smart an' clever an' he shore had a way with the women folks. But mebbe I got somethin' he didn't have, Mary. I've allus loved yuh, better'n anythin', even life itself. He didn't. He loved 'imself first, last an' allus, an' he wasn't the kind tuh play fair with just one woman. He had tuh have variety."

He paused again, but it was only for a moment.

"I've learned a heap, Mary. I kin understand a heap o' things now that I didn't savvy before nohow. Y'know things look diff'rent once yuh've had a chance tuh study 'em out, an' I reckon I've had plenty o' time fer that. An' I'm dumb enough tuh remember what I've learned, too. Come home with me, Mary."

"Pat—please!" she pleaded. "Don't say any more. I can't stand it!"

"Awright," he said heavily, "if that's the way yuh feel 'bout it."

He turned slowly toward the door, but he halted suddenly and tossed his hat aside, retraced his steps swiftly, gripped her shoulders and swung her around.

"I ain't takin' no fer an answer," he said determinedly. "I ain't goin', an' that's final—'less you come with me, y'hear? Yuh're still my wife an' I still got the right tuh take care o' yuh. 'Course I'm willin' tuh admit it took me a heck of a long time tuh get wise tuh things. 'Stead o' standin' by like a danged fool an' waitin' fer yuh tuh come back by yoreself, I shoulda come after yuh a long time ago. I know I shoulda stopped the goin's-on between you an' John right off. I knew he didn't mean well by yuh, but I didn't wanna do anything tuh hurt yuh or interfere with yuh long's what yuh were doin' was what yuh wanted tuh do."

She was sobbing openly now. He caught her to him and held her close, and she did not resist.

"We've both made mistakes, Mary—we wouldn't be human if we didn't—but we don't hafta make any more. Now I don't wanna hear or say 'nother word 'bout it. We're goin' home—tuhgether."

She wanted to raise her head to tell him how she had learned to hate John Sears, suavity, smile and all; how quickly his "charm" had worn off; how cold, ruthless and grasping he really was. She wanted to tell him how she had prayed for him to come for her, how her courage had deserted her on the several occasions when she had started for the saloon, prepared to face him and humble herself and plead with him to take her back. There were so many things she might have told him—the very things he would have delighted in hearing. But this was not the time for such telling, nor even for begging forigveness. Pat held her tightly, and she gloried in his strength.

There was so much of him; his bulk gave her what she had missed the most—someone stalwart to cling to, someone strong and steadfast to turn to when her courage wavered and faltered and needed bolstering. And now her happiness was reflected in her tears.

There was a warm smile on Pat Donlin's face. He was happy now—happier than he had ever been before.

Mary was coming home again.

Doran stood watching four men busily engaged in building a new bunkhouse. Reynolds had provided the lumber and the carpenters. The railroad had more cut lumber than it could use—so he had insisted—and as for the men—well, they weren't doing anything anyway. The framework had gone up quickly; now the last of the wallboards was being nailed into place. The boards which would become the sloping roof had already been cut and were stacked against the front of the building. The lumber was new and clean, and the structure, incomplete though it was, glistened with a strange brightness on the fire-blackened site on which the former bunkhouse had stood.

Doran turned slowly when he heard a light step behind him. It was Ann Miller, grave and thoughtful. She halted beside him presently.

"Will they be finished with it by sundown?" she asked.

"If they keep hustlin' like they are now—why, shore," he replied. "Y'see, Ann—I've been pushin' 'em 'cause them punchers Donlin recommended oughta be showin' up here 'long 'bout evenin', an' if the bunkhouse is ready fer 'em, they kin move right in an' get a night's rest so's they kin get started on things 'round here first thing in the mornin'."

She was silent for a moment.

"When must you leave?" she asked.

"Me? Oh, there ain't no perticular hurry. 'Nother day or two won't make much diff'rence, one way or another," he said casually. "I'd kinda like tuh see things movin' along like they oughta before I pull out. Say, how 'bout you an' Donlin? Yuh got things all fixed up between yuh?"

She nodded her answer.

"Wa-al?" he asked, intimating a desire to know some of the details of the agreement.

"Well," she began in an almost disinterested tone, "since we own the property on both sides of the Pass and since the vein appears to be one, we've agreed to pool our interests and work both sides jointly."

"Sounds awright so far, but what about the railroad? Kinda busts right through things, don't it?"

"No, not exactly. Strange as it may seem, the vein stops when it reaches the Pass. It's solid rock there, Mr. Donlin tells me. Then, curiously enough, it reappears on the Bar-M side."

"Shore is curious awright. Reckon nature musta figgered on the Pass bein' used fer a railroad some day, so it kinda took care o' the situation, eh?"

"Yes."

"The hull set-up sounds fine tuh me, Ann. Doggone, reckon you'll be just about the richest woman 'round these parts."

There was no answer. He watched her out of the corner of his eye.

"Dan."

"Yeah?"

"Captain Reynolds told me about my father," she said.

He grinned boyishly.

"Oh, yuh mean 'bout what we done the other night?" he asked.

"Yes."

"Shore made me feel glad tuh hear that it was yore Dad's heart that was tuh blame fer what happened—'stead o' my bullet."

She smiled wanly and turned away, then halted again presently.

"Dan, do you like working for Mr. Burnham and Captain Reynolds so very much?" she asked.

He shrugged his shoulders.

"Oh, I dunno. They ain't the worst tuh work fer—not by a long shot. 'Course I'm willin' to admit it's on'y a job, but heck—I don't aim tuh go on workin' fer a boss forever. I'm lookin' for'ard tuh the day when I'll be able tuh buy me a small place an'—"

"Settle down—perhaps get married?"

"Oh, I'll settle down awright. As fer me gettin' married—wa-al, that's somethin' else again. I'm afraid the girl who'd have me ain't been born yet."

They heard a clatter of galloping hoofs and turned just as Captain Reynolds and Matt Burnham swept into view. The horsemen halted a moment to look over the new bunkhouse, then swerved away and pulled up in front of them.

"Howdy," Reynolds said. He nodded toward the bunkhouse. "Seems tuh be comin' along."

"Shore is," Doran replied.

"I'm very grateful to you, Captain," Ann said, "and to you too, Mr. Burnham. You've both been very kind and generous with your men and your lumber."

"That's awright," Reynolds told her.

Burnham grunted.

" 'Course. Ferget it," he said. He eyed Doran. "So, yuh're quittin' the railroad, eh? Figger yuh'll be able tuh boss a ranch this size an' a wife at the same time?"

Ann's eyes widened. She turned quickly toward Doran, but he flushed and hastily averted his eyes. Reynolds jerked Burnham's coat sleeve, but the railroad man paid no attention to it.

"Yuh're gettin' a fine-lookin' girl, young feller," he went on. "Mighty fine-lookin'. How soon yuh plannin' tuh get hitched?"

Doran coughed to cover his embarrassment. But it was a weak effort—more of a wheeze than a cough. He tried it again. He did better the second time—in fact, he did so well that he almost choked. Reynolds did his best to avoid looking at him.

"Don'tcha think we oughta be gettin' on, Matt?" Reynolds asked quickly. "If yuh still wanna get tuh town tuhday an' take care o' everythin' there that needs 'tendin' to an' make it back tuh camp in time fer supper, reckon we'd better be makin' tracks."

Burnham eyed him curiously.

"Who said anything 'bout goin' tuh town tuhday?" he demanded. "An' how come yuh ain't told me before this 'bout things needin' 'tendin' to there, huh?"

"Reckon I musta plumb fergot about 'em," Reynolds said lamely. "But now that I've remembered 'em, if we was tuh get goin' pronto, mebbe we could do what we had tuh an' still get back tuh camp before nightfall."

The railroad man frowned. He considered for a moment and finally shrugged his shoulders.

"Wa-al, awright," he said begrudgingly. "If we gotta go, reckon we might's well go now an' get it over with."

Reynolds' face reflected his relief. He wheeled his mount.

"So long," he called over his shoulder. "Comin', Matt?"

He loped away. Burnham shook his head.

"Never knowed such a changeable feller," he said.

He spurred his horse and clattered off. Reynolds twisted around in his saddle and looked back. He reined in presently, waited for Burnham to join him; then, together again, they galloped away toward McCloud.

Doran followed them with steely eyes.

"Danged fools," he muttered. "Blabbed like a couple o' ol' women. I shoulda knowed better'n tuh confide in 'em."

He frowned and turned away and toyed with his gun-belt, opened the buckle and closed it, opened it again and closed it again. Ann's eyes shone with a new and strange brightness. She watched him patiently, quietly. Finally he swung around and raised his head.

"Go on," he said miserably. "Say it."

"Say what, Dan?"

He gestured impatiently.

"You know—'bout what a gall I had fer ever imaginin' that a girl like you'd marry a danged fool like me," he said dully. "Go on an' say it. I kin take it."

"But I don't want to say it," she said gently. "I—I don't feel that way about it at all."

His eyes widened.

"Huh? Yuh don't? Yuh mean—" His voice trailed away. He stared at her incredulously, unbelievingly. "Ann, yuh can't mean it—you wouldn't marry a feller like me!"

"If he were to ask me to, Dan—well, I might."

He caught her in his arms.

"Ann," he whispered huskily, "I'm askin' yuh—will yuh marry me?"

"Dan—those men over there—they're looking!"

"Let 'em look," he said happily. He kissed her eagerly, hungrily—a second time, too. "Long's it's me who's doin' this an' yuh're the one I'm doin' it tuh—shucks, honey, let 'em look!"

THE END

www.ingramcontent.com/pod-product-compliance
Lightning Source LLC
Chambersburg PA
CBHW052008240626
47153CB00008B/2788